Young Heroes
❖ ——— of the ——— ❖
CONFEDERACY

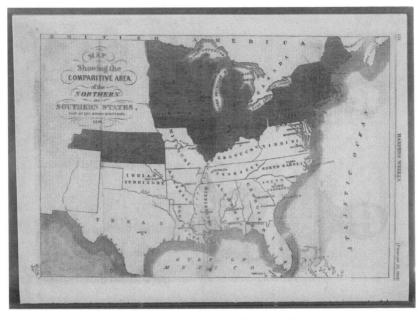

The Confederate States of America. (Library of Congress)

Young Heroes
⋅∗⋅————— *of the* —————⋅∗⋅
CONFEDERACY

By Debra West Smith

PELICAN PUBLISHING COMPANY

Gretna 2012

The word "Pelican" and the depiction of a pelican are
trademarks of Pelican Publishing Company, Inc., and are
registered in the U.S. Patent and Trademark Office.

Library of Congress Cataloging-in-Publication Data

Smith, Debra, 1955 June 16-
  Young heroes of the Confederacy / by Debra West Smith.
    p. cm.
  Includes bibliographical references and index.
  ISBN 978-1-4556-1684-8 (pbk. : alk. paper) -- ISBN 978-1-4556-1685-5
(e-book) 1. Children--Confederate States of America--Biography--Juvenile
literature. 2. United States--History--Civil War, 1861-1865--Children--Juve-
nile literature. 3. United States--History--Civil War, 1861-1865--Participa-
tion juvenile--Juvenile literature. I. Title.
  E585.C54S65 2012
  973.7083--dc23
                            2012017748

Printed in the United States of America
Published by Pelican Publishing Company, Inc.
1000 Burmaster Street, Gretna, Louisiana 70053

To my husband,
Chef Curtis,
for his patient support
and wonderful meals

Contents

Acknowledgments

Research is a treasure hunt. Without tips, clues, nuggets of wisdom, encouragement, and good directions, this book could easily have lost its way. My heartfelt thanks go to:

- My family and friends who listened patiently
- Editor Nina Kooij, for her belief in the project
- Aunt Eliza and Jerrie Dent, who came along for the rides
- Beth Coker, who introduced me to the Confederate navy
- Martha Boltz of the *Washington Times*
- Jennifer Bittner and the staff of Hanger Orthopedic Group
- Jasper Burns, Bryan family historian
- Sue B. Moore, a long-lost cousin, for sharing her knowledge of Texas and Mississippi
- Rick Frederick, archivist, Caswell County Historical Association
- John Storey, descendant of John Baptist Smith
- Terry Reimer, director of research, National Museum of Civil War Medicine
- Elizabeth B. Dunn, David Rubenstein Library, Duke University
- Beverly Rude, author of *Sam*
- Anita Teague and the staff of the Sam Davis Home
- Maurice C. York, assistant director, Joyner Library, East Carolina University
- Frank Arre, Naval Historical Foundation
- Ward Calhoun, Lauderdale County Archives
- Vanessa Burzynski, Texas Division, United Daughters of the Confederacy
- Warren Stricker, Panhandle-Plains Historical Museum
- Scott Thompson, historian, Laurens County Historical Society
- Robert Gates, Florida Division, Sons of Confederate Veterans
- James Hayward, Martha Sue Skinner, and Michael Collins, Collins family historians
- Ron Kolwak, archivist, *Tampa Tribune*
- Brent Moore, photographer of SeeTN.com
- Sarah Murphy, Camden Archives and Museum

Introduction

Why write another book about the Civil War? A library could be filled with volumes about this tragic chapter in America's history, which is still debated and called by many names. To debate it again is not my purpose.

It's been said that "life is 10 percent what happens to us and 90 percent how we respond to it." Young people of the 1860s were swept up in trouble not of their making. How they responded to it was the ultimate test of character. No Southerner was spared hardship, and patriotism and a sense of adventure drew countless boys and young men into the conflict. Honor and defense of homeland kept them there, despite suffering and the unexpected horrors of war.

The girls and young women who were left behind dealt with hunger, home invasion, and heartache as they waited for loved ones to return. Some recorded their experiences in diaries and letters. In addition to hard work and nursing the wounded, they found creative ways to support their soldiers. They were heroes as well.

The choice of whose stories to tell has been difficult! Most will be unknown to you. Their backgrounds vary, as do the contributions they made. I hope you will find inspiration in the courage and resiliency of these young heroes.

Young Heroes
of the
CONFEDERACY

Chapter 1

JAMES EDWARD HANGER

The war in Virginia had just begun. Men of all ages were called upon to defend their homes and country, the new Confederate States of America. They came from all walks of life, many from families who had never owned a slave. For boys and young men who had not seen the face of war, it was an exciting time. They had no clue as to the suffering that lay ahead.

James Edward Hanger was eighteen, a sophomore at Washington College in Lexington, Virginia. Jim, as the family called him, was studying to be a mechanical engineer. When the war started, he went home to Mount Hope Farm, near Churchville, Virginia. He tried to enlist in the army but was turned down because of his age. Jim's parents, William and Eliza Hanger, tried to convince their youngest boy to stay in school. There had been no land battles at this point, and most soldiers were just sitting around campfires. However, the Hangers knew that war was a dangerous business.

Jim was determined. Though his parents were unhappy with the choice, he joined an ambulance corps taking supplies to the Churchville cavalry. Two of his older brothers were already part of this unit, so Mrs. Hanger packed food and clothes for them as well. Jim caught up with the group in Philippi. The commander, Colonel Porterfield, was trying to build an army of 5,000 men in western Virginia. His goal was to protect the railroad.

Ambulance corps. (Library of Congress)

NEW RECRUIT

The colonel found that people there were not ready to get involved, and he had few volunteers. Jim was allowed to join the small group of untrained, poorly armed men. It was June 2, 1861, and they were not prepared to face the army marching to meet them.

When news reached Philippi that 4,500 Federal soldiers would arrive that night, the result was panic. Colonel Porterfield knew it would be useless to face them with his 750 men. He ordered them to pack up and be ready to move at a moment's notice. Then it started to rain, a hard, driving rain that lasted all night. Thinking the enemy would not travel in such conditions, the colonel waited.

Most of the volunteers did not have tents and slept wherever they could find shelter. Jim and a few others stayed with the unit's horses in a barn. To pass the time, the volunteers climbed into the loft and jumped in the hay, while pickets stood guard outside. Finally, everyone settled down for the night.

THE PHILIPPI RACES

Jim's turn at guard duty came in the early hours of June 3. As he waited for daybreak, a loud gunshot pierced the air. Two cannon thundered in response, echoing across the sleeping town as smoke rose from the hill above. Marching through the dismal rain, the Federals had arrived and taken position during the night. The first land battle of the Civil War had begun. Jim raced inside for his horse and belongings as the other men tumbled out. Suddenly a cannonball exploded through the barn wall! It struck the hard ground and ricocheted upward. Jim was raising his foot to mount when a pain like nothing he had ever known tore through his body. The dreadful six-pound cannonball had shattered his leg. . . .

Outside was chaos as Confederate soldiers slipped between Federal lines to head south. Some were captured and the injured left behind. The short skirmish would be remembered as "The Philippi Races," for the speed of their escape.

A barely conscious Jim tried to hide by dragging himself into the hay. He grew weaker as his useless leg bled. Four hours later, the soggy Federal soldiers rode into Philippi. Fortunately, Jim was not well hidden. They found him that day, lying among the shattered oak boards and blood-soaked hay.

Dr. James Robinson of the Ohio Volunteers was called. He knew that the only way to save Jim's life was to remove the damaged leg quickly. The youth was very weak, with a huge chance of infection.

Federal soldiers removed the barn door from its hinges and set it on two stacks of hay to make a table. Dr. Robinson had never performed an amputation, but he did the surgery in forty-five minutes. There was no anesthesia.

Jim's leg was amputated seven inches above the knee. After the surgery, he was taken to a church in Philippi, which served as a hospital. Then he was cared for by a family in their home and later in another hospital. There he was given a "pegleg," a heavy piece of wood shaped like a peg. Using it was like trying to walk with a table leg, painful and awkward.

Back Home

Two months passed before Jim was part of a prisoner-of-war exchange.

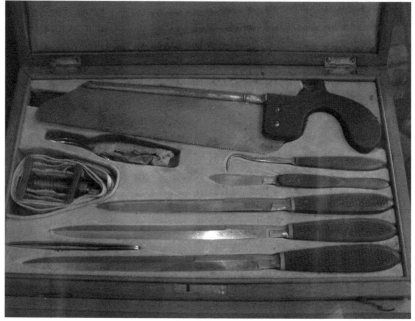

Amputation kit. (Courtesy of Sam Davis Home)

Finally, he could go home. Instead of letting his family comfort him over his loss, Jim wanted to be alone. They tried to understand, thinking he needed time to adjust to his handicap. His mother brought meals to his door and later picked up the empty plate. Sometimes they heard him thumping around upstairs and knew he was all right.

Records show that over 400,000 trauma patients were treated on the Union side, and at least 30,000 were amputations. In the 1860s, it took only two years to become a surgeon, and most doctors had never amputated a limb before going off to war.

When Jim asked for willow wood from the trees outside, and barrel staves, his family humored him. At night he placed buckets of shavings outside the door, which they replaced with new wood. The family couldn't imagine what he was carving, but working with his hands was good therapy.

Three months passed. One day there was a new sound on the

stairway. It was like a dream of the old days—Jim walking down the stairs! Where was the painful clomping of his dreadful peg? What had brought about this miracle?

During his three-month exile, young Jim had used the barrel staves and willow wood to build the world's first articulated, double-jointed prosthetic limb!

HELPING OTHERS

Jim Hanger was the first of 60,000 men who would lose a limb during the Civil War. When news of his invention reached the papers, other amputees asked about his device. He moved to Richmond and set up shop, always looking for ways to improve the leg. In 1863, he applied for a patent. Before the war ended, the state of Virginia presented him a contract for 1,000 prosthetic limbs.

With business doing well, Jim married Nora McCarthy in 1873. They had six sons and two daughters. All the boys grew up to work in their father's company. He moved it to Washington, D.C., and then opened branches across the United States and into Europe. In 1915, Jim toured Europe to learn about new techniques in surgery brought on by World War I. He enjoyed the outdoors, played golf, and invented new

James Hanger. (Courtesy of Hanger Orthopedic Group)

How was the Hanger limb better than other artificial legs?

1. Comfort—carved to the match the length of the other leg, and fit perfectly, it weighed less than five pounds.

2. Function—with two hinged joints and a little practice, it allowed a person to walk almost normally.

3. Appearance—constructed from lightweight wood, with a carved foot, the Hanger limb made it possible to wear a shoe or boot.

Early Hanger workshop. (Courtesy of Hanger Orthopedic Group)

things—venetian blinds, the water turbine, and a toy horseless carriage for his children.

For many years, Jim served as an elder in the Presbyterian Church and was known for his kindness and good humor. Going to work one day, he noticed an elderly black man begging on the street. The man had lost both legs. Jim took him to the shop and fitted him with Hanger limbs. They became good friends, and Jim gave him a job.

When Jim died in 1919, the Hanger Company had over 1,000 employees in forty-three states and several countries. It is still helping people . . . and a very special dolphin named "Winter." Her prosthetic tail, as seen in the movie *Dolphin Tale*, was developed by Hanger employee Dan Strzempka and financed by the company. Today, the glue known as "WintersGel" is being used for artificial human limbs.

I know your feelings and problems, but the world is just as beautiful as of old. The flowers and the trees, and the sunshine, are just as precious as ever. Nor has opportunity fled. Science and invention have done, and are doing, more to cancel your misfortune than can possibly be done for any other serious handicap in life.

—James Hanger

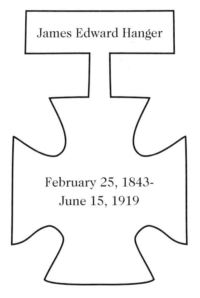

James Edward Hanger

February 25, 1843-
June 15, 1919

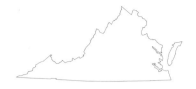

Chapter 2

John Randolph Bryan

When Virginia left the Union in May 1861, Richmond soon became the capital of the Confederacy. It was only 100 miles from the Federal capital in Washington. Fighting was fierce as Union forces tried to capture Richmond.

War has always encouraged new technology. The Civil War saw the first use of the submarine, torpedo, and ironclad ships. And a recent invention found a practical use—the hot-air balloon!

French scientists had launched the first hot-air balloons in 1783. Later, a few daring Americans flew balloons as entertainment. Early in 1861, Prof. Thaddeus Lowe proved his theory of a west-to-east jet stream by flying from Ohio to South Carolina. However, the flight took place just as America was going to war. His plan to cross the Atlantic next was cancelled. Instead he offered his services to the military. Most of the Union generals thought ballooning was silly and expensive. How could it help them win the war?

The answer was surveillance, much like our satellites today. From the air, Lowe could watch Confederate camps and troop movements. Pres. Abraham Lincoln approved the idea, and Lowe became America's first "high-flying spy."

The Confederates were upset! There was no hiding from a spy in the sky. They tried to fool him by setting up "dummy" cannon and camps. Blackouts were ordered, with no campfires allowed. This hurt morale as the men complained about eating cold food. They tried to shoot the balloon as it ascended each morning, but it quickly went out of range. Spies

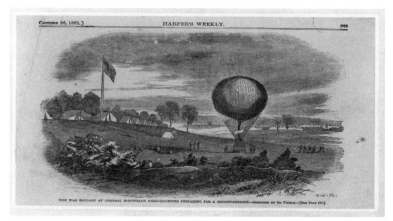

THE WAR BALLOON AT GENERAL M'DOWELL'S HEAD-QUARTERS PREPARING FOR A RECONNOISSANCE.—Sketched by Ed. Forbes.—[See Page 687.]

War balloon at Union general Irvin McDowell's headquarters. (Library of Congress)

Prof. Thaddeus Lowe observing a battle. (Library of Congress)

slipped into the Union camp at night, hoping to destroy Lowe's well-guarded balloon. This also failed. There was another solution—a balloon of their own.

Hot-air balloons were made of silk and filled with illuminating air (hydrogen gas). Since both were costly, the Confederates found a cheaper way—a huge cotton bag coated with tree resin to make it airtight. It was filled by capturing the heat from large bonfires. Since hot air rises, the balloon would also rise and stay afloat until the air cooled. Hopefully, it would be long enough to see what the enemy was up to.

VOLUNTEER

But who would fly it? The only experienced aeronauts were on the Union side. Gen. Joe Johnston sent a request for a volunteer to do reconnaissance on the peninsula near Yorktown, Virginia. His message was received by a young aide in Gen. J. B. Magruder's office. Though many soldiers in the field would have gladly traded places with him, Capt. John Randolph Bryan, working for his cousin at headquarters, was ready to prove himself. Scouting in enemy territory sounded like an adventure to the twenty-one-year-old. It was also a chance to see a sweetheart who lived behind enemy lines.

As friends tried to discourage him, Ran (his family's nickname for him) rode off to meet with General Johnston. At first, the general was skeptical. Did this tall, dark-eyed boy have enough experience to be a good observer?

Ran, who had grown up in that part of Virginia, convinced the general that he knew the countryside well. He could also tell the difference between the branches of service. However, he did not know that he would be observing from the basket of a hot-air balloon. Perhaps in the interest of secrecy, General Johnston had failed to mention that. Convinced that the young captain could do the job, the general described his mission.

Ran sprang to his feet. "Sir, I will gladly go anywhere on horseback and get the information you want. However, I have never even seen a balloon!"

The general was firm. "I have plenty of scouts. What I need is a man in a balloon, and that is your duty. Prepare to go on my order," he said.

High-Flying Spy

Ran bowed and walked out as bravely as he could. Members of the balloon squad showed him how to manage the balloon and signal with a wigwag flag. The order came the next day—April 13, 1862. Half a mile from Confederate lines, behind a thicket of pine trees, the squad lit a hot fire of pine knots and turpentine. When the balloon had filled with hot air, it was sealed off. Ran, with a notebook and pencil in his pocket and his heart beating wildly, climbed into the basket. Using a windlass, his ground crew began to let out the half-mile of rope that controlled the balloon.

Slowly the balloon rose from behind the treetops, visible to the Yankees. Ran watched the excitement as they hurried to aim cannon his way. . . . *Boom!* Shells and bullets whistled by in a dreadful music. Ran frantically signaled the men below to let the rope out faster. Soon he was out of firing range and could breathe freely again. Knowing that the balloon would only stay aloft while the air was hot, he quickly went to work. Ran described the scene this way:

> From my elevated position I could see the whole country in every direction. A wonderful panorama spread out beneath me. Chesapeake Bay, the York and the James rivers, Old Point Comfort and Hampton, and the fleets lying in both the York and the James, and the two opposing armies lying facing each other.
>
> I therefore took out my note-book and made a rough diagram showing the rivers, the roads and creeks, and marking where the different bodies of the enemy's troops were upon this little map, using the initial "I" for infantry, "C" for cavalry, "A" for artillery, and "W" for wagon trains, and I marked down about the number of troops that I estimated at each point.

The balloon slowly rotated like a top as he wrote. Finally, Ran signaled to pull it down. There was another rain of bullets but without damage. General Johnston was very pleased with the information and congratulated young Captain Bryan. Ran asked for permission to return to his old job.

The general refused, saying, "My dear sir, I fear you forget that you are the only experienced aeronaut that I have!"

The squad was soon ordered to make a second flight. It was much like the first, with a team of galloping horses added to pull the balloon down faster. Ran had also been given a new nickname—Balloon Bryan.

NIGHT FLIGHT

On May 4, the night before the Battle of Williamsburg, the squad was ordered to send the balloon up again. General Johnston wanted to know which way the enemy was moving. A nearly full moon brightened the countryside. Ran hoped that he wouldn't be seen and shot at this time.

As the balloon glowed in the firelight, a large crowd gathered to watch the show. One soldier got too close and stepped into a coil of the rope. The balloon rose, yanking the rope and wrapping it around his leg. The man screamed. His friend grabbed an axe and quickly chopped the rope to free him.

About two hundred feet in the air, Ran felt a hard jerk. The freed balloon sailed upward, as if pulled by a great force. He trembled, helpless to stop his "runaway steed." So he hung on, wondering how high and how far it would fly. Finally, the balloon reached its equilibrium and hovered over the Confederate army.

The wind rose after awhile, carrying Ran and the balloon over enemy lines. What if it came down there? Capture was what he feared most—spies were often shot, and prison camp was even worse. It would be better to be dumped into the York River.

Instead the balloon slowly drifted as it cooled, back to the Confederate side. Ran realized that he was several miles from the launch site. The troops camped below were from Florida and knew nothing about a Confederate aeronaut. Thinking he was a Yankee spy, they chased the balloon, trying to shoot it down. Ran shouted, but no one heard him amid the rain of bullets.

Once again, the wind picked up, shoving the balloon and its terrified pilot over the York River. Though narrow in some places, it was three or four miles wide at that point. The balloon cooled, dropping close to the water as Ran prepared for a swim. He tried to fold his six-foot frame into a sitting position, but the basket was too small. The tall, well-oiled boots he was so proud of would have to come off. As he pulled and tugged at them, the balloon's dangling rope splashed in the water. Ran grabbed his pocketknife and cut the boots off.

He was about to jump out when a sudden breeze pushed the balloon onshore and into an apple orchard. What joy to stand on solid ground! Ran tied the balloon to a tree and found a farmhouse. Though bitten by the farmer's dog, he was given a horse for the eight-mile ride back to camp. With the information the reluctant aeronaut had gathered, General Johnston prepared for the coming attack.

It was Captain Bryan's last flight. He fought in that battle and others, respected for his courage and clear thinking under fire. When the war ended, he married Margaret Minor and had nine children. Their son would one day write about his parents' kindness and hospitality.

Ran never lost his adventurous spirit, always ready to try a new idea or invention to make farm life easier. His growing family had more labor-saving devices than anyone they knew. Since Ran lived until 1917, we can only imagine what he thought of airplanes!

John Randolph Bryan

January 9, 1841-
December 27, 1917

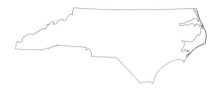

Chapter 3

John Baptist Smith

I n times of war, communication is everything. Long before satellites and cell towers, ancient people around the world used smoke signals to send simple messages over a distance. Samuel Morse proved in 1835 that signals could be transmitted by wire, and the telegraph was born. Then Albert Myer, an army surgeon in New Mexico, invented a way to send coded messages using flags and torches.

When the Civil War began, the Confederacy jumped on the latter idea. Their Independent Signal Corps trained a special group of young men to send messages in code. A battlefield could spread out for miles, so knowing your enemy's strength and position could make the difference in life or death, victory or defeat.

Signal officers had to be in good physical shape, intelligent, brave, and able to keep secrets. Their codebook was important information that could not fall into enemy hands! And it was not a job for men afraid of heights. In order to see clearly—and be seen— they perched on wooden towers, buildings, trees, and mountaintops. Many

A signal officer's kit included:

- Seven flags of different sizes and colors
- Four hickory poles, four feet long and jointed like fishing rods
- A copper torch
- A canteen and service can for carrying a torch and lantern fuel
- A case and haversack for storage
- A funnel, pliers, wormer, and shears for filling and trimming torches
- A codebook
- A telescope or binoculars

signal officers were killed or had their equipment blasted away. Fog and smoke rising from a battlefield made their task even harder.

John Baptist Smith spent his first seventeen years in Caswell County, North Carolina. He was raised on a farm called Hycotee and was a student at Hampden Sydney College when the war erupted. He quickly joined the "Milton Blues," Company C of the Thirteenth North Carolina Volunteers.

Soon John was promoted to sergeant and chosen for training in the new Signal Corps. His brother William and poet Sidney Lanier were also part of this hand-picked group. They operated signal and observation posts along the James and Appomattox rivers.

John Baptist Smith. (Courtesy of John Storey)

John witnessed his first battle on a warm spring day in March 1862. The Confederate ironclad *Virginia* (formerly the USS *Merrimac*) made a bold run to Hampton Roads, Virginia, where Union warships blocked the entrance to the harbor. It was also the first battle using the new iron-plated ships. The *Virginia* destroyed two wooden Union ships and damaged another.

The Union's ironclad, the *Monitor,* arrived the next day. The two ships dueled for three hours but neither was badly

Confederate sailors aboard the Merrimac, *loading cannon during combat with the* Monitor. (Library of Congress)

damaged. The *Virginia* finally steamed back upriver to its homeport, and the *Monitor* stayed to continue the blockade. Young John and his mates may not have realized it, but naval warfare had just changed forever. The beautiful wooden ships of the past were no match for the homely iron-plated vessels. Shipbuilders in France and England took note and began using the new technology.

In order to see the signals from a distant station, the Signal Corps used powerful telescopes. The best at that time had 30x magnification. Signalmen claimed that, using telescopes on a clear day, they could read flag signals from stations up to twenty miles away. Using binoculars, they could observe signals about ten miles away.

New Invention

In July 1862, John was placed in charge of the station at Fort Fisher, on the Cape Fear River in North Carolina. His job was to improve communication between two forts at the mouth of the river. Confederate ships trying to run the blockade

Ironclad gunboats, also called rams, were made by putting iron plates over oak beams. They could withstand cannonballs and ram a wooden ship with a sharp bow shaped like an axe head. Since iron was scarce, it was salvaged from the railroad, cooking pots, and farm tools.

there needed to know when the coast was clear. The wigwag system used flags on long poles that were waved in a coded pattern. At night, torches or lanterns, moved in the same manner, replaced the flags. A foot torch was used as a reference point. The "Flying Torches" were impressive but hard to see in the blowing wind and ocean spray. John pondered the problem, later noting, "One day while in the ordnance department of the Fort, I chanced to spy a pair of ship starboard and port lanterns, and this thought flashed into my mind, 'Why not, by the arrangement of a sliding door to each of these lanterns, one being a white, the other a red light, substitute flashes of red and white lights for the wave of torches to the right and left, to form a signal alphabet and thus use the lanterns at sea as well as upon land?'"

John shared his idea with the commander, who sent him to a machine shop. His lanterns were presented to a group of naval officers for approval. They were so impressed that a pair of John's lanterns and a signal officer were ordered for each ship trying to run the blockade!

More signal stations were placed along the coast. The blockade runners came in close to shore at night and flashed a light toward the signal station. The station could signal back that enemy vessels were near or that it was safe to enter the harbor.

The new lanterns worked so well that a British ship's captain wanted to take John to England, where he could apply for a patent. John refused, not willing to desert his country in her time of need. As reward for John's valuable contribution, the secretary of war offered the signal officer his choice of vessels on which to serve. He chose the blockade runner *Advance,* perhaps the fastest ship afloat.

THE *ADVANCE*

No life could be more adventurous and exciting than life aboard a

Night signaling. (Library of Congress)

blockade runner. John, who was now nineteen, went aboard in May 1863. The *Advance* soon had another young recruit, sixteen-year-old James Sprunt. He was glad to have a friend like John, who would recall, "It was my first separation from home and as we prepared to turn in for the night by the light of a carefully screened lamp I was deeply impressed by the moral courage of Johnnie Smith, who in the presence of several onlookers, evidently caring nothing for these things, quietly got out his Testament, read the evening chapter and then upon his bended knees commended his soul to Him who had confidence in those afar off upon the sea. That simple act of worship, under circumstances peculiarly trying to a young man, not only strengthened me for my duty, but made an impression for good which has never been effaced."

The *Advance* crew would soon need a great dose of courage. For two nights, they had tried to slip into the Cape Fear River with badly needed supplies. Fog was too thick the first night; the second night, they were chased off to sea by Federal vessels. The third day was clear. The men rested and tried to hook one of the sharks that circled the ship. Coal was running low,

> In 1862, an estimated two thousand blockade runners slipped by the U.S. Navy to enter Confederate ports.

and the captain's barometer told him a storm was on the way.

That night, they tried again to enter the river. The shore was just in sight when a sudden lurch nearly knocked the men off their feet! They were trapped, stuck on a sandbar. Though the engines strained to move her, the *Advance* sat helpless against the coming storm. When it arrived, the waves could pound her to pieces.

At daylight, the signal station onshore relayed her situation. Steamboats came from twenty miles upriver to unload the *Advance*, before the storm arrived or the enemy found her. As the last steamer prepared to leave with its precious cargo, the *Advance*'s captain spoke to his crew: "Shipmates, from my experience at sea, I am satisfied we are on the verge of a great storm and feel it my duty to you to say it is very doubtful about the ship, in her helpless condition, being able to live through the night, but I am determined to stand by her and would like for as many of you to stay with me as will do so voluntarily; but it must be entirely of your own free will. And those of you who do not care to take the risk are at liberty to go ashore on that boat."

A few of the men chose to stay, including young John.

"Jump aboard the boat, my lad, and go ashore," the captain told him.

John said, "Captain, I alone can communicate with the shore, and I think I ought to stay with you."

"My lad, 'twill be impossible for any help to reach us from the shore. You have a father and mother to live for; jump aboard the steamer or it will be too late."

In his mind, John saw the faces of his family—his parents, who depended on him as the oldest son, and the little sisters and brothers who looked up to him. It seemed that at that moment, his whole life hung on a scale of destiny. Would he choose home and life, or duty and death?

"Captain, I thank you for your consideration but feel it my duty to stay with you," said John. "I will stand by the ship, and if she goes down, I will go down at the post of duty."

A tear trickled down the brave old captain's cheek. "God bless you, my lad. I would be proud of such a son!"

The riverboat steamed away, leaving the men on the *Advance* to meet their fate. John quietly slipped down to his stateroom to pray, commending his loved ones at home, himself, and his shipmates to God's protecting care. He returned on deck, happy that he had chosen the path of duty. Years later, he described the storm:

The sea had become one vast mirrored surface, not a breath of air to ripple its placid serenity. With notes of warning the sea birds had taken their departure. . . . Strange, weird sounds, the groans of the mighty deep came to our ears. A great wave, the skirmish line of the dreaded foe, bears down upon us in one unbroken swell, strikes our ship on her starboard quarter and forces her stern squarely to the sea, from her former position.

"Thank God for that!" exclaimed the Captain. "Now my lads, if we can keep her stern to the shore there is a chance for our lives. Stand by all hands to hoist sail!"

Messages for loved ones are exchanged between shipmates as they pass to their allotted posts of duty, when all becomes still. Our cheeks burn as with the heat of a furnace; we pant for breath; the suspense is dreadful!

The little cloud grows greater and greater, approaches faster and faster, gathering strength and velocity as it comes, until the sea and clouds mingle in dense, struggling, writhing masses, and with the speed of the whirlwind and roar of the tornado this allied force of wind, water and darkness burst upon us, howling and shrieking through the ship's rigging.

In spite of all, the staunch craft, though wrenched and twisted by the violence of the waves and knocks against the land, held together, and after a night of mingled hopes and fears, daylight found her lying safe and sound in the placid waters of the Cape Fear.

The storm, which seemed destined to destroy the bonnie ship, was made the instrument of her preservation. She was carried upon the crest of the waves across several hundred yards of shoals, over which, otherwise, it would have been impossible to have gotten her to reach the channel of the Cape Fear River.

The rising sun gilded the clouds with gold, they vanished; smiled upon the winds, they abated; kissed the waves, they subsided; and converted a night of darkness, terror and suspense into a day of light, safety and joy. Oh! That men would praise the Lord for His Goodness and for His wonderful works to the children of men.

The *Advance* and its crew survived, and John was promoted to lieutenant. That summer, he was sent to Petersburg to command the signal lines from Gen. Robert E. Lee's headquarters. The assignment was a huge compliment for such a young soldier. When the general surrendered, John secured paroles for his signalmen. On April 15, 1865, exactly four years after he enlisted, John went home.

Seven years passed. John married Sabra Annie Long, and the couple had nine children. In addition to farming, they ran a mill, post office, and general store. Years later, John wrote about his wartime adventures for family and friends. They were published in local papers, as was the news of John and Annie's fiftieth anniversary!

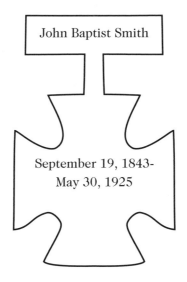

John Baptist Smith

September 19, 1843-
May 30, 1925

Chapter 4

SIMON BARUCH

Being Jewish has never been easy. Born in Schwarsenz, Prussia (now Poland) in 1840, young Simon Baruch inherited his father's thirst for learning. He was a good student and wanted to be a doctor. But even if he studied medicine, Jews in his country were not allowed to practice. Simon knew that he would soon be forced into military service and was faced with a huge decision.

Mannes Baum, a friend of the Baruch family, had recently immigrated to America. He wrote letters describing the freedom and opportunities for a young person willing to work hard. He offered Simon a place to live and a job in his general store in Camden, South Carolina. Simon made his decision. After a cold winter voyage, he arrived in America on December 23, 1855.

Simon was grateful to the Baums, who treated him like a foster son. However, he was more interested in reading books than helping customers. Mr. Baum sent him to work as an apprentice to a local doctor while he learned English.

In November of 1860, Simon moved to the beautiful city of Charleston to attend medical school. Tuition was fifteen dollars per course, and he signed up for seven classes. Since doctors had less to learn in those days, only two sessions were needed to graduate.

> There were hazards to being a medical student. Studying anatomy meant examining the bodies of people who had died. In the years before rubber gloves, a scratch on a hand invited germs. Several students died each year of diseases picked up this way.

A few days after Simon's arrival at medical school, Charleston caught "secession fever." When the legislature called for a convention to discuss it, the city celebrated with parades and fireworks. However, Simon's long days of study left little time to worry about politics. His weekends were filled with athletics and social events.

On April 12, 1861, the bombardment of Fort Sumter shut down the school as professors joined the army. Simon pondered what to do. What was this war to him? Was it about the right to secede or to own slaves? Would the fighting really be over in a few months, as some people believed?

Growing up in war-torn Europe had taught him that conflicts could go on for years. The Medical College of Virginia was still open, so he moved there. As capital of the Confederacy, Richmond was an exciting place. It was also home to the new Chimborazo Hospital, the largest military hospital of its time, with over eight thousand beds.

As the first year of the war raged on, Simon studied hard. He graduated in March 1862. At age twenty-one, having never treated a sick person, he was now Dr. Baruch!

OFF TO WAR

The military was desperate for doctors. Simon realized how much he owed his new homeland. "South Carolina gave me all I have," he said. "I'll go with my state." He enlisted and was made an assistant surgeon. The position paid $110 a month. It was a lot of money for that time, but his uniform cost $200. With dark wavy hair and pale blue eyes, Simon looked dashing in his gray suit and green silk sash. Black trim and stripes on the pants helped distinguish doctors from other soldiers.

Simon was assigned to Kershaw's Brigade of the Army of Northern Virginia, and his job was to keep 500 infantrymen healthy. His first battle experience was at Second Manassas. It was there he learned that a strange, mosquito-like, whizzing sound meant that a Minié ball was flying too close! Dodging them, he found a sheltered place to care for the wounded.

Simon awoke the next morning to the true horrors of war. Dead and

More than ten thousand Jews fought for the Confederacy. Rabbi Korn of Charleston said, "Nowhere else in America . . . had Jews been accorded such an opportunity to be complete equals as in the old South." Gen. Robert E. Lee allowed his Jewish soldiers to observe all holy days, while generals Ulysses S. Grant and William T. Sherman issued anti-Jewish orders.

wounded men were everywhere. At the field hospital, a surgeon was about to remove a patient's shattered limb. Seeing Simon's pale face, he offered the knife, saying, "Perhaps you would like to operate, Doctor."

The Minié ball inflicted bone-shattering injuries that infected easily.

An estimated 600,000 men fought for the Confederacy—50,000 were killed by the enemy, while 150,000 died from disease.

In July, Simon's brigade marched into the fighting at Boonsboro, Maryland. He was told to stay with about seventy-five wounded men who had to be left behind. Quickly making an operating table out of two barrels and a door, he went to work. As bullets flew outside, the Confederates retreated and blue Federal uniforms filled the streets. Simon and his patients were taken as prisoners of war.

Two months passed. The Confederate doctors were allowed to care for their patients, working side by side with the Union medical staff. Finally, they were released. Simon was back with his unit when it fought at Chancellorsville the following spring. During his long hours of surgery, his right eye began to bother him.

Kershaw's Brigade reached Gettysburg on July 1. The battle lasted three days; over half of the men from South Carolina were killed or injured. Around 14,500 Union soldiers were wounded, and 6,000 Confederates.

For doctors and nurses, it was a heartbreaking test of endurance. Simon worked thirty-six hours straight, tending men from both sides. At sundown on July 3, he tumbled into a pile of hay and slept. When he awoke, the Army of Virginia was gone. A shell exploded nearby as Union

Citizen volunteers assisting the wounded. (Library of Congress)

cavalry rode in. The doctors quickly raised a yellow flag, the symbol for hospitals. Simon was once again a prisoner of war.

The prisoners were taken by train, in an open cattle car, to Fort McHenry in Baltimore. Though the doctors received better treatment than other prisoners at the fort, they worried about the flies and worms in their soup. It was a cold autumn day when they were finally released.

THOMASVILLE

The following July, Simon was promoted to "full surgeon." The sight in his right eye was growing worse. Afraid of losing it completely, he asked for a leave of absence. After two months rest, he was assigned to hospital duty in North Carolina. He got there just in time to evacuate the patients—General Sherman's men were marching north, destroying everything. The wounded men were loaded into cold, crowded train cars and taken inland to Thomasville. Some died on this miserable journey.

It was Simon's job to set up a new hospital and care for the patients before more of them died. The men of Thomasville helped clear out factories and churches to make room for beds. They gathered pine straw, which schoolgirls stuffed into sacks for mattresses. A message came, warning that 200 more wounded were coming on the next train. Simon went from house to house, asking women to prepare bread, bacon, and

Simon Baruch. (Courtesy of Camden Archives and Museum)

gallons of coffee. Some of the ladies helped in the hospital as well.

After the new patients were settled, Simon slept for two hours, then spent another long day in surgery. His head began to pound, and he fell unconscious, a victim of typhoid fever. For the next two weeks, he was delirious, and the other doctors thought he would die. When he finally awoke, General Lee had surrendered. The terrible war was over.

When he was strong enough to use crutches, Simon went home. The journey to South Carolina took him through a wasteland. J. K. P. Blackburn, a Confederate soldier from Texas, described the scene:

> The ravages of war were fearful to behold. . . . Every living animal for use or food was taken from the citizens, including all kinds of fowls, and their smoke-houses and pantries were stripped. . . . There was just one article of food they could neither destroy nor carry off and that was sweet potatoes, of which there was an abundant crop the season before.
>
> Of all the campaigns made during the Civil War by either Northern or Southern armies, none had more of devastation and cruelty and inhumanity than this one led by W. T. Sherman across South Carolina. . . . And no other campaign equaled this one for its barbarity except perhaps Sherman's march from Atlanta to the sea . . . he said he had made Georgia realize that war was hell and that he had devastated a country fifty miles wide and two hundred miles long so completely that if a crow visited that section he would have to carry his rations with him or starve.

The Baum family welcomed Simon, but they were suffering as well. The state was still occupied by Federal troops. There were no railroads, bridges, or mail service and little money. Though Simon was ready to open a medical practice, who could afford to pay him?

The one bright spot in his life was Belle Wolfe, Mrs. Baum's niece. However, courting her posed a problem—what did he have to offer? Belle's family was descended from the Sephardim, European Jews who had come to America during the colonial period. They had prospered in the New World and could find a better match for their daughter.

LIFE IN NEW YORK

Simon decided to seek his fortune in New York. He arrived in the autumn of 1865, only to find that the city had enough doctors. Hospital positions were hard to find. Opening a private practice with no money or social connections was next to impossible. He agreed to volunteer at the North-West Dispensary, a free clinic for people who could not afford medical care. It was located in Hell's Kitchen, a part of Manhattan that was known as one of the worst slums in America.

If life had been difficult in the war-torn South, it was hardly better for residents in the tenements. Most of these buildings had four stories and a cellar. Each story was divided into four dark, stuffy apartments. Four families shared a single faucet and sink in the hallway. Privies (toilets) were outside.

For a few months, Simon lived in a tenement as well. He became convinced that clean habits, better food, fresh air, and sunshine would prevent many diseases. Doctors in the 1860s were just beginning to emphasize these issues. He spent many hours in the libraries and hospitals, soaking up new ideas from men who were experts in their field.

In the spring of 1866, Simon realized that working without pay was bringing him no closer to his goals. He returned to Camden, found patients among the freed slaves who still worked on plantations, and took whatever they offered as payment—chickens, vegetables, sewing, laundry service, and hay for his horse.

Finally, young Dr. Baruch could afford a home. He married Belle and began writing articles for medical journals. Always seeking new ways to prevent disease, he pushed for laws that made smallpox vaccinations available to all children in South Carolina.

In 1880, Simon was ready to try life in New York again, this time with Belle and their four sons. With a respectable résumé, he set up private practice and continued to research and write. Recalling his months in the tenements, he started a campaign for free public rain baths (showers) across the city. It took years, but the idea spread to Chicago and other cities across the country.

Simon was one of the first doctors to insist that removing a diseased appendix was the best way to save a patient's life. He also traveled Europe to learn more about hydrotherapy, which uses hot and cold water to relieve fever and pain. It was the beginning of physical therapy.

Another event that put Simon's name in the news involved a brilliant young musician named Josef Hoffmann. The eleven-year-old was praised as the greatest child pianist since Mozart. He was brought to New York by an agent who pushed him to perform forty concerts in one month. Josef's health was suffering, and Simon was asked to examine him.

He advised that the boy should be released from the contract and allowed to rest. While newspapers questioned Simon's judgment, and the child's father argued with the agent, Josef stayed with the Baruch family. He slid down banisters with their boys, went on calls with Simon in his buggy, and generally had a fine time. Josef got well.

Though they lived in New York, the Baruch family remained loyal Southerners. Belle joined the United Daughters of the Confederacy, and if a band struck up "Dixie," Simon would jump up and give the Rebel yell—even at the Metropolitan Opera House.

One of the sons who slid down the banister was Bernard, who became an advisor to Presidents Woodrow Wilson and Franklin Roosevelt.

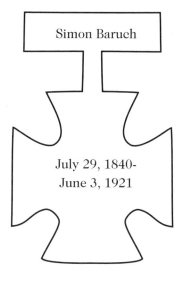

Simon Baruch

July 29, 1840-
June 3, 1921

Chapter 5

HARRIET BAILEY BULLOCK

Arkansas in the 1860s was a peculiar blend of the Wild West and *Gone with the Wind*. Settlers had spilled across Tennessee, Mississippi, Arkansas, and Texas, like water from a ruptured dam. Planters from the East brought their families, slaves, and dreams of rich farmland. Many settled in southern Arkansas, which favored the Confederacy. Folks in the Ozarks were more likely to support the Union.

Fighting in the Border States began years before the first shot was fired at Fort Sumter. To the west lay Kansas, a non-slave state. Raiders known as Jayhawkers made it their business to free as many slaves as possible, even if it meant killing farmers and burning their property. There were constant skirmishes with the Border Ruffians, Southern sympathizers from Missouri. The western part of Arkansas bordered Oklahoma, the new Indian territory. Tribal leaders were also divided over secession. When the Civil War started in 1861, Native Americans fought on both sides.

The fires of hatred were fueled by acts of revenge as both sides struggled for control of the frontier. Guerrilla bands, called partisan rangers, were not part of the Confederate army but worked to make life miserable for Federal forces. This environment hardened some young men, who grew up with little respect for the law, or human life.

> The outlaw Jesse James joined Quantrill's Raiders at age fourteen, after Union soldiers attacked his family on their Missouri farm.

BUILDING A PLANTATION

In 1848, Col. Charles Bullock brought his wife, eight children, slaves, and farm equipment to Dallas County, Arkansas. Rich soil along the Ouachita River was ideal for cotton. Two hundred acres of forest was quickly cleared, and crops were planted. A sturdy log cabin was built. The place was called Sylvan Home.

More daughters were born to the family, including Harriet Bailey Bullock in 1849. Mrs. Bullock died when Bailey was three, so the girl was raised by an older sister and Aunt 'Liza, a slave who served as nursemaid. A few years later, Pa married again, and the family continued to grow. The Bullock children were taught to treat all adults, including their slaves, with respect. Bailey called the men uncles and the women aunts.

Humans have an amazing ability to adapt to their circumstances, whatever they might be. Diet is a good example. Whether we grow up eating snails in France, sushi in Japan, or crawfish in Louisiana, the foods we know are what we consider to be "normal." Anything else seems strange to us. Change requires courage, an open mind, and time.

So it is with social customs. In modern times, white Southerners often wonder how their ancestors, known from their diaries and letters to be moral people, could tolerate slavery. From their writings, it is clear that many disliked the practice or thought of their servants as extended family. Slavery had been around for centuries and for them was "normal." However, some families disagreed about owning slaves and how they should be treated. Changing a society, and the way people thought, would take radical surgery—a painful, bloody mess.

As a child, Bailey loved exploring the woods and playing with her younger brother, sisters, and the slave children. Aunt Rose's cabin served as a daycare center for the mothers who worked in the fields. Among Bailey's happiest memories were scooping peas with a mussel shell from Aunt Rose's large pot as the peas cooked over a fire in the yard. Sometimes she caught minnows from a stream and brought them for Aunt Rose to fry. The men who hunted might bring in deer meat, bear, or even a beaver tail. At night, they often heard wolves howl.

Romping outdoors gave Bailey a healthy appetite, and she never felt satisfied after meals with the family. Young ladies were supposed to eat in moderation and keep their waistlines tiny. One older sister suffered from ribs that had grown to overlap, caused by wearing a tight corset. The younger girls were allowed two biscuits for breakfast, a small piece of bread with meat and vegetables for dinner, then milk and bread for supper. At Aunt Rose's, however, Bailey could eat all she wanted. Aunt 'Liza also told her years later, "I have to laugh about your going bare headed. We just couldn't keep a bonnet on your head and sometimes would have to hunt all over the place for your bonnet liable to find it under the house or anywhere in or out of the yard."

Education was important to the Bullocks. After being homeschooled until she was ten, Bailey joined the older children in walking two and a half miles to the log schoolhouse. There were sixteen other students of various ages in Dr. Steel's class. Discipline was strict, and children might be switched for almost any reason, such as reading their lessons incorrectly.

It was the same at home. Though Bailey's father could be tender with his children, everyone tried to avoid him when his temper flared. Once night he came home from hunting, tired, sick, and irritable. Something was wrong with the coffee, and he struck their beloved cook with his horsewhip. Bailey, hearing the commotion from upstairs, bolted from her bed to find them in the dining room. She grabbed her father's hand, screaming, "You shan't whip Aunt 'Riah! You shan't whip Aunt 'Riah!"

Surprised by his daughter's outburst, and perhaps ashamed of himself, Colonel Bullock stopped. As far as Bailey knew, Aunt 'Riah was never punished again.

War on the Frontier

The war came to Bailey's world when she was eleven. She didn't fully understand what "states' rights" and "secession" meant but knew that something was dreadfully wrong. Though a loyal Southerner, her father was unhappy about Arkansas leaving the Union. Bailey's oldest brother, Tom, joined the army when the fighting started in Virginia. Soon soldiers arrived from Texas and camped near the farm. Some had measles and were brought to the Bullocks for care, since the family was immune.

As Federal forces came up the Mississippi River, the Confederate government ordered that all the cotton be destroyed. If the South could not get its valuable crop to market, it would make sure no one else did. However, Colonel Bullock decided to hide his cotton—in the woods, the kitchen loft, even the meat house. The Yankees never found the hundred bales, which helped support the family when the war was over.

With the river blockaded, clothes and shoes became precious and hard to replace. A new schoolteacher, Miss Mary Cooper, agreed to work in exchange for a room, food, and clothing. When she moved in with the Bullocks, the plantation shoemaker made her a pair of leather shoes from buggy cushions. Old dresses were remade into a new one for the teacher, and a bleached palmetto hat was woven for her, just like the family wore. In exchange, she gave the children music lessons.

When his eighteenth birthday drew near, Bailey's brother Kim (Kimbrough) left to join the army in the East. A lonely ache filled her heart as the family waited for letters from their two young soldiers.

Then on April 18, 1864, the boom of cannon was heard! The Battle of Poison Springs, just miles away, had begun. As the Confederate army retreated, soldiers trudged into the yard, so hungry that they dug bread from the mud where Aunt 'Riah had thrown it to the ducks.

More soldiers came—some bleeding and all hungry. Soon the armies under General Shelby and General Marmaduke were camped on the plantation. The house was turned into a hospital. Bailey helped scrape lint from a tablecloth to dress wounds. She was impressed by the generals, who sat on the porch and talked with her pa. The presence of so many hungry, ragged men was a trial to some of the family. Anything might go missing when no one was looking—a piece of chicken from the kitchen, fabric from the loom, or a horse from its stall.

When the army finally moved on, acres of land had to be cleaned and garbage burned. Bailey found one treasure among the items left behind—a book of Shakespeare! She loved reading and added it to her cherished collection, which included *Robinson Crusoe*.

Military encampment at plantation house. (Library of Congress)

FORAGERS AND THIEVES

Two wounded men stayed longer, until they were well enough to travel. One Sunday morning, Colonel Bullock left the house quickly, taking them along. Suddenly twenty or thirty Federal soldiers rode into the yard, their bright blue uniforms flashing. They searched for any Confederates left behind, asked for food, and rounded up the farm's remaining horses. Bailey's sister Honey cried as her pony, Fanny, was led away; a kind officer told the men to return it. Old Joe, one of the mules, decided not to join the Union army, and no one could force him past the gate. The following spring, Joe and Fanny plowed the field for planting.

Colonel Bullock returned and learned that his horses had been stolen. He followed the soldiers to their camp and did

> William F. Cody, later known as Buffalo Bill, described his regiment (the Second Kansas Cavalry) as "the biggest gang of thieves on record."

not come home that night. The family fretted, wondering what the enemy might do to their outspoken father. However, he returned safely the next day. He had caught the commander in a generous mood and was paid for the horses.

Many farmers were not as fortunate when foraging soldiers came around. In the effort to feed, clothe, and provide horses for thousands of men, foragers from both armies were sent out to find whatever they could. They swarmed through the countryside like a plague of locusts, leaving angry, starving citizens behind.

Families grew creative in finding places to hide their food and live-stock. A small calf might be shoved into the fireplace, which was covered in the summer when cooking was done outside. Money could be hidden in a beehive, or cows and hogs in the forest.

EMANCIPATION

As the Confederate army lost ground in the Border States, Colonel Bull-ock tried to prepare his family for the changes emancipation would bring. Bailey had grown up with a maid to tie her shoes, brush her hair, hang up her clothes, and make sure she wore a sunbonnet outside. Now she learned to take care of her own needs, and much more.

Bailey was fifteen when the war ended in the spring of 1865. When their freedom came, many of the slaves stayed and worked until harvest, then received a portion of that year's crop. To begin their independent life, some married or went to live with other family members. Others stayed to work as paid laborers.

Bailey wrote later:

> I loved the servants. So far as I ever saw, during the four years of the war (and as I sympathized with the Negroes, they expressed themselves more freely before me than the others), I never heard any hint of rebellion. There was nothing but thor-ough loyalty to "Master" and their "white folks." They were dependent on us and we depended on them. There was no trou-ble until the matter was settled that they must be freed and then both white and colored united in claiming the freedom granted by the Proclamation of Emancipation; for slavery had bonds of

servitude and responsibility for white people as well as for the Negroes.

BOARDING SCHOOL

A new chapter opened in Bailey's life when she and a sister left to attend boarding school in Arkadelphia. Along with a trunk of clothes, they took flour, meal, 200 pounds of meat, and five gallons of lard to help pay tuition. It was a rough journey in a wagon drawn by oxen.

While at school, Bailey learned not only to fix her hair but to flirt with the young men who stopped by. She was having a fine time until news reached her of brother Kim's death back in North Carolina. He had not died in battle but of a fever while in camp. The grieving sisters were allowed to go home and were there to greet brother Tom when he returned. It was a bittersweet reunion with the young veteran, who refused to talk about his experiences in the war.

Tom was soon visited by a friend from North Carolina. Bailey never forgot her first meeting with handsome Nat Daniel. His kind smile and twinkling black eyes would remain etched in her mind.

Harriet Bailey Daniel. (Photo in Harriet Bailey [Bullock] Daniel Papers, David M. Rubenstein Rare Book & Manuscript Library, Duke University)

When their two years at boarding school were complete, it was planned that Bailey and her sister would go on to college in Alabama. The first leg of their journey was by steamboat up the Mississippi. What an exciting voyage it was! They stopped in Memphis to visit with two married sisters. It was there that sister Kate changed the course of Bailey's life by convincing her that Pa could not afford the tuition this time. He was growing old and frail, and the farm was struggling.

Bailey understood. Instead of going to college, she took a teaching job in Tennessee. She wrote Nat often. As other beaux came and went, she continued to cherish his letters. After two years of teaching, Bailey went home. She stayed there, learning to cook, wash clothes, and other tasks of running a household.

On January 24, 1872, Bailey married Nat Daniel, who took her to his home in North Carolina, called Tranquility. They had seven children and spent the rest of their lives there. In 1917, Bailey received a letter from her old nurse, Aunt 'Liza:

Witherspoon, Ark
Mar 19th '17

My Dear Miss Harriett
    I have thought of you often, so often & wish that I could see you again. Charlie was here a few days since & he gave me your address. I am well am living with a family named Howard. . . . I am a widow but have a good home with the Howards. Miss Harriett I wish you would please tell me my age . . . I have but one child, a daughter, lives about a mile from me. I will be so glad to hear from you. I feel young & am very little gray & everybody says I look young & I sure am taking the very best of care of myself now. I wish you would please write to me for I will be overjoyed to hear from you. I used snuff for a good many years but it was injurious to me & I quit it absolutely six years ago and haven't touched it since.
    With much love and best wishes always I am your

Old Slave Gal
Eliza Bullock

Bailey cried when she read the letter and was happy to answer it. At age seventy-five, she wrote a poem about the fifty-two slaves she knew as a child, recalling the names of each one.

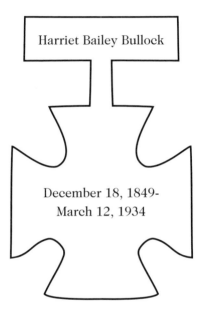

Harriet Bailey Bullock

December 18, 1849-
March 12, 1934

Chapter 6

JESSE AUSTIN HOLMAN

Texas was a wild place when Jesse Holman was born there in 1842. His mother, Nancy Burnam Holman, was possibly the first Anglo child born in Stephen F. Austin's famous colony of 300 families. She died when Jesse was six years old. His father, George, grew cotton in the rich prairie soil of Fayette County, near the Colorado River.

Even as the Kiowa, Apache, and Comanche nations fought to keep what remained of their land, Southerners who had migrated to Texas voted to secede from the Union. Three-fourths of them did not own slaves but strongly resented Northern domination.

About ninety thousand Texans served the Confederacy, two-thirds of them staying in the Southwest. They fought against Union invasions in the Red River, New Mexico Territory, and Rio Grande Valley and to protect their harbors. Trade with Mexico made the blockade easier to bear in Texas than in other Confederate states. In return for cotton, Texans received military supplies, medicines, iron products, food, coffee, and tobacco.

The main Union attack on the Texas coast was aimed at the state's largest seaport, Galveston. On October 4, 1862, a small Union fleet sailed into Galveston harbor with 4,000 troops. They planned to land near Sabine Pass and capture Galveston. Forty-seven men, mostly immigrant dockworkers, used six cannon to hold them off in an amazing victory.

Mexican Americans were bitterly divided over which side to support. About 2,500 *Tejanos,* as they were called then, fought for the Confederacy and 950 for the Union.

Horse Soldiers

Most Texans preferred to serve in the cavalry. A British officer noted that "it was found very difficult to raise infantry in Texas, as no Texan walks a yard if he can help it." Southerners loved horses, and boys learned to ride as soon as they could walk. Since most towns had a racetrack, Southern horses were bred for their speed and smooth gaits.

Southern boys also loved to hunt! The excitement of stalking deer and turkey, chasing foxes, and trailing raccoons at night—in all kinds of weather—prepared many young men for the hardships they would endure as soldiers.

Up North, where roads were improving, people were learning to depend on wheels. Most horses there were larger, heavier, and used for farming. A captain in the Tenth New York Cavalry wrote about his new command:

> Such a rattling, jingling, jerking, scrabbling, cursing, I never heard before. Green horses—some of them had never been ridden—turned round and round, backed against each other, jumped up, or stood up like trained circus-horses. . . . Some of the boys had never ridden anything since they galloped on a hobby horse, and they clasped their legs close together, thus unconsciously sticking the spurs into their horses' sides.

While Union soldiers were still learning to ride and use a saber, swift Confederate cavalry units were on the move. They burned bridges, cut telegraph lines, captured supplies, and raided behind enemy lines.

Some of the Texas volunteers joined armies in the East. When Col. Benjamin Terry came to recruit soldiers, Jesse and his cousin Nat joined the Eighth Texas Cavalry. Over 1,100 volunteers (mostly young single men) composed the group known as Terry's Texas Rangers.

Wondering what lay ahead, the recruits traveled north to become part of the Army of Tennessee. This began a four-year campaign that took them

> Each volunteer was expected to bring his own shotgun, revolver, Bowie knife, saddle, bridle, and blanket. Unlike most units, the Rangers were provided with horses.

A member of the Eighth Texas Cavalry. (Courtesy of Don Troiani)

across seven states and into around 275 battles, such as Shiloh, Fort Donelson, Chickamauga, Cumberland Gap, Stones River, and Kennesaw Mountain. Terry's Rangers became known as one of the finest cavalry units in the war's Western theater.

Members of Terry's Texas Rangers. (Courtesy of Panhandle-Plains Historical Museum, Canyon, Texas)

During their first winter, the Rangers suffered more from the weather than from the enemy. They had left home in late summer, and many did not bring winter clothing. The commissary was not able to meet the needs of so many soldiers. Without warm clothes sent from home, they would have suffered greatly. They also caught the measles.

Soldiers sometimes supplied their needs by trading with the enemy. One Ranger, James Blackburn, described a time when they were camped on the Tennessee River:

> The pickets talked to each other across the stream and found out they were somewhat acquainted. They arranged for a truce, a suspension of hostilities until they could have a swim, a few yarns, swap tobacco for coffee, exchange newspapers and have a good time generally.
> These truces were common in all parts of the army when it could be arranged without a commissioned officer being present. . . . I

believed then, and I still believe now, if the terms of peace had been left to the men who faced each other in battle day after day, they would have stopped the war at once on terms acceptable to both sides (except the civil rulers) and honorable to all alike. These men that always bore the brunt of battle never had and never will have any bad feelings towards each other.

STONES RIVER

Christmas of 1862 found the Army of Tennessee, led by Gen. Braxton Bragg, camped near Murfreesboro, Tennessee. They were only thirty miles from Union general William Rosecrans' army in Nashville. General Bragg hoped to block the path to Chattanooga and protect the farms of Middle Tennessee that were supplying food to his men. As Bragg's army began to move, Jesse was promoted to full sergeant.

General Rosecrans left Nashville on December 26 with 44,000 men to meet Bragg's 37,000 soldiers. Though rain, sleet, fog, and Confederate cavalry, slowed them down, they reached the Stones River three days

Pickets trading between the lines. (Library of Congress)

later. By the evening of December 30, 1862, both armies faced each other in the fields and forests near Murfreesboro.

While the generals plotted, the men tried to sleep on the cold mud and rocks. The bands of both armies played tunes to raise their morale. Sam Seay of the First Tennessee Infantry recalled the night:

> Just before 'tattoo' the military bands on each side began their evening music. The still winter night carried their strains to great distance. At every pause on our side, far away could be heard the military bands of the other.
>
> Finally one of them struck up 'Home Sweet Home.' As if by common consent, all other airs ceased, and the bands of both armies as far as the ear could reach, joined in the refrain. Who knows how many hearts were bold next day by reason of that air?

At dawn the next cold morning, as the Federals ate their breakfast, General Bragg's men attacked. The Rangers attacked the Union left flank, hoping to cut the supply line from Nashville. Jesse led twelve men around the far left, behind enemy lines. Their orders were to bring a battery of six guns that had been captured back to the Confederate lines. Smoke billowed from the many cannon, whose thunder rolled like an unending storm. It was heard forty miles away.

The dense smoke made it impossible to see members of the Third Kentucky Cavalry until they were surrounded. Jesse and his men were captured, along with his horse, pistols, and a fine fifty-dollar Spanish blanket.

PRISONER OF WAR

As Jesse learned what it meant to be a prisoner or war, the terrible battle raged for two more days. On the Union side, over thirteen thousand were killed or injured at Stones River. The Confederates counted more than ten thousand casualties. Many of the wounded died later. In the end, General Bragg withdrew from Murfreesboro, to fight again another day.

Freezing rain added to the misery of prisoners marching to Nashville and confined for nine days in an old house. They would have starved if

CHARGE OF THE FIRST BRIGADE, COMMANDED BY COL. N. B. WALKER, on the FRIDAY EVENING OF THE BATTLE OF STONE RIVER.

Battle of Stones River. (Library of Congress)

the local ladies had not sent boxes and baskets of food. Two prisoners escaped on the terrible trip to Chicago, and many suffered from frostbite. Years later, Jesse recalled the bitter cold:

> On the boat taking us to prison were 800 prisoners. We stopped at St. Louis, and we were marched up in the city and formed in two lines facing a two-story hotel where the officer in charge made us a speech, promising us liberty, anywhere inside the lines, if we would take the "Oath of Allegiance."
>
> When he was through he ordered all who would take advantage of the offer to step two paces to the front. The proudest moment of my war experience was when only two of that 800 ragged, starved and frozen bunch stepped to the front.
>
> Then several ladies, who were on the upstairs porch, waved their handkerchiefs and cried out "Stand to your colors, God bless you; we love to see you do it!"
>
> Then came up out of that two feet of snow the "Rebel Yell" from those 800 throats, and a loud huzza for "Jeff Davis and the Southern

Confederacy." Our answer to the Yankees was that we would rot and starve before we would take the oath, and many did.

The prisoners arrived at Camp Douglas, a large training camp and prison. It sat in a low area that turned into a sea of mud with each rain. The barracks were poorly constructed and unsanitary. In February 1863, 10 percent of the camp's prisoners died. Jesse, who as a soldier had never been sick or missed roll call, survived the bitter winter. Three months later, he was released in a prisoner exchange.

The Rangers had ridden from Texas with 1,100 men, but at the war's end, only 175 were left. Though Jesse had many close calls, he was never wounded. In 1867, he married Mary Evelyn Folts and had a family of seven children. He worked in real estate, was a leader in the local chapter of Confederate Veterans, and died a week before his eightieth birthday. Jesse never forgot his comrades or the amazing feats of Terry's Texas Rangers.

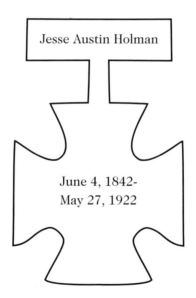

Jesse Austin Holman

June 4, 1842-
May 27, 1922

Chapter 7

SAMUEL DAVIS

I magine a world with no telephones, texting, or e-mail. In the 1800s, communicating with someone at a distance was painfully slow. Letters and messengers could take weeks. Invention of the telegraph helped, but in wartime, lines could be cut. Since commanders needed information quickly, they sent soldiers out as scouts and couriers. Many lives, and the outcome of a battle, could depend on knowing what the enemy was up to.

Scouts gathered information about roads, bridges, and troop movements. These daring soldiers were usually young, single, and excellent horsemen. Since they often worked behind enemy lines, they needed to be calm and resourceful as well. Scouts wore their military uniforms and, if caught, were often treated like other prisoners of war.

Scout's gear. (Courtesy of Sam Davis Home)

Spies gathered information in a different way. They wore civilian clothes or perhaps the enemy's uniform. A spy might give a false name, become friendly with enemy soldiers, and send messages in code. The Confederate Secret Service grew into a huge network. A spy could be anyone who sympathized with the other side. Since some Northerners believed that the Federal government should not force states to remain in the Union, they were willing to help the Confederates. A captured spy's punishment was death.

We don't know what young Samuel Davis wanted to be when he grew up, but it probably wasn't a scout. He was born in 1842 and raised as part of a large family on a farm near Nashville. Charles Davis had several children with his first wife and then nine more with his second wife, Jane! Sam was Jane's first child and very devoted to her.

In this full house, Sam would not have been lonely. He was close to brothers John and Oscar and a young slave who was given to him as boy. Coleman Smith Davis was two years younger than Sam and came to the

Sam Davis's boyhood home.

farm when Sam's father bought his parents. According to Coleman, he worked in the fields with Sam, plowing and hoeing.

Sam attended a local school until he was eighteen. He was a kind, serious young man, always quick to help a smaller boy who was being bullied. Though Sam was supposed to continue school at the Western Military Institute in Nashville, he refused unless his brother could go. The dispute with their father was so sharp that Sam left home for awhile. Finally, his father agreed. Sam went to Nashville in January 1861, with Coleman along as his body servant.

TENNESSEE VOLUNTEERS

When the war started that spring, cadets like Sam became drillmasters. In May, he joined the Rutherford Rifles, also known as Company I of the First Regiment, Tennessee Volunteer Infantry. Sam served with them for two years. That autumn they marched to Virginia and took part in Gen. Robert E. Lee's first campaign of the war. Then they joined Stonewall Jackson's forces for a miserable winter in the Shenandoah Valley. Icicles formed on the men's clothing and gear, and many soldiers suffered from frostbite. Some even died from the cold.

While Sam was in the east, the Union army invaded Tennessee. By gaining control of the Memphis-to-Charleston railroad, they could cut off supplies that the Confederacy needed. The First Tennessee marched home through heavy rains, muddy roads, and swollen creeks. They arrived as over eighty thousand men gathered for battle near Shiloh Church. On April 6, the weather cleared. The Confederates surprised the Yankees by attacking early that morning. The Battle of Shiloh raged for two days and left almost twenty-four thousand soldiers dead or wounded.

Sam was slightly wounded at Shiloh. His regiment moved on to fight in Corinth, Mississippi and Perryville, Kentucky, where he was wounded again. By Christmas, they were camped on the Stones River, just a few miles from his home. The cold days between Christmas and New Year's saw another terrible battle, this time for control of Murfreesboro, Tennessee. At least thirty-seven thousand soldiers were wounded or killed.

The Confederate army then retreated south, where they spent the next six months.

COLEMAN'S SCOUTS

Sam was invited to join Coleman's Scouts that summer. His brother John was already part of this group of thirty soldiers. They were led by Capt. Henry B. Shaw, a spy who dressed as a rumpled old doctor peddling herbal remedies.

The life of a scout was exciting for an adventurous young man. Information was gathered by watching troop movements, talking with soldiers on the road, and from citizens. Ladies going through Federal lines learned all they could. Some befriended the Federal officers.

In Nashville, a special tree served as a "post office," where papers and letters could be stashed. Packages were hidden across Middle Tennessee in rocks and hollow trees. Scouts picked these up for Captain Shaw, who rewrote documents in code and signed them *E. Coleman*. Riders then took the information to Decatur, Alabama and Chattanooga, Tennessee.

Sam's servant, Coleman, was with him on these journeys. Once, they barely escaped as Federal troops chased them through the woods and into a cornfield. Sam outsmarted them and got away. Another time, they burned a wagon train of Yankee ammunition.

Despite their hardships, the soldiers found time for recreation. Once about a hundred of them played an enormous game of leapfrog!

Sam and Coleman slept anywhere and ate whatever they could find. Whenever possible, Southern sympathizers gave them shelter and a hot meal. Among these was the Patterson family. Kate Patterson and her cousin, Robbie Woodruff, went often to Nashville for newspapers, medicine, and supplies for the scouts. After the war, Kate married Sam's brother John. Some thought that Sam and Robbie were sweethearts.

Northern newspapers often printed information that Union commanders would have preferred to keep secret. Southern generals couldn't wait to read the news!

LAST MISSION

The Yankee commander General Dodge was determined to stop Coleman's Scouts. He assigned over one hundred soldiers from Kansas, known as the Jayhawkers, to round them up. Tension grew as one scout after another was captured or killed.

One November night, Sam, with Coleman, arrived at home cold, hungry, and barefoot. His mother closed the curtains so that no one would see him. She made Sam's supper while his father fixed a pair of boots. They gave him a Federal coat that his brother had found and their mother had dyed brown using walnut hulls. Much of the Confederate army wore homemade uniforms of different colors.

Sam went to the Patterson home next, getting food and supplies from Kate. He and Coleman left with the Jayhawkers on their heels. Finally, he met with Captain Shaw, who gave him a "large mail" to deliver—newspapers, a map of defenses at Nashville, and important letters for

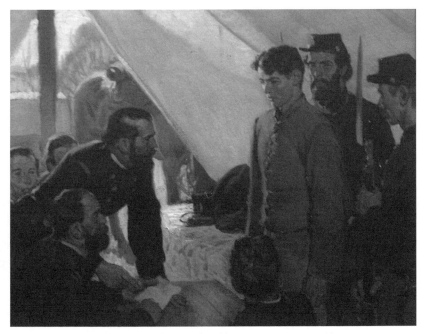

Interrogation. (Painting by Harold Von Schmidt)

General Bragg in Chattanooga. He was stopped on the way by two men in Confederate uniform. Sam realized too late that it was a disguise and tried to get away. One man grabbed his horse. Sam and Coleman were captured.

Captain Shaw was arrested and placed in the same jail. In the days that followed, they pretended not to know each other. General Dodge questioned Sam about Coleman's Scouts, offering to spare his life for information. Sam insisted that he was a scout—not a spy—and refused to identify anyone. Coleman, Sam's body servant, begged Sam to allow him to say that the man they really wanted was sitting in the other cell. Sam refused, and Captain Shaw remained silent.

LOYAL FRIEND

Staying loyal to his friends and homeland, Sam was sentenced to death. He said, "I would rather die a thousand deaths than betray a friend." After spending time with the chaplain, and writing a letter to his mother, Sam was executed on November 27, 1863. John Doak, a Federal soldier, wrote home about the event:

> The Genl offered to pardon him if he would tell who gave him the information but this he refused to do. Just before going onto the scaffold the chaplain asked him if he had not better tell. This seemed to insult him. Said he, "Do you think I would betray a friend? No I would die a thousand deaths first."
>
> I stood near by him as I could get for the guard. He died like a soldier. A brave boy he was—though a spy. I almost hated to see him die. I guess he was 21 years of age, hair, eyes and complexion dark, five ft. 8 inches high and weighed about 150 lbs. Samuel Davis was his name.

Coleman was released and went home. After the war, he married and had a dozen children. Afraid that the Yankees would punish him as a spy, he waited almost sixty years to apply for a veteran's pension. Finally, Coleman told his story of growing up and riding with Sam. He spoke of the young master's kind, generous nature and how losing Sam broke his heart. He was given a small pension.

Sam's statue at Giles County Courthouse, Pulaski, Tennessee. (Courtesy of Brent Moore/ SeeMidTN.com)

Davis home dressed in mourning.

Sam received the Confederate Medal of Honor. Years later, statues of Sam were placed at the Tennessee State Capitol and the courthouse square in Pulaski, where he died. General Dodge, who ordered Sam's death, contributed to one of them.

A third statue stands at his school, now Montgomery Bell Academy, where students sign the old registry that bears Sam's name. The young men who attend are challenged to live by the same high standards of honor and loyalty.

Sam's home in Smyrna, Tennessee is visited by countless schoolchildren, who learn about life in the 1860s, and the "Boy Hero of the Confederacy."

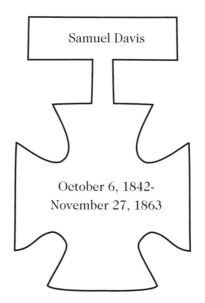

Samuel Davis

October 6, 1842-
November 27, 1863

Chapter 8

Emma Sansom

Long before Europeans came to America, the Cherokee people roamed the Southeast. Then waves of settlers, wars, and treaties forced them from their land. Many Cherokee tried to adapt by taking on the white man's lifestyle—houses, clothing, education, and the Christian faith. But while some considered the Cherokee good neighbors, greedy men still wanted their land.

In the 1830s, Pres. Andrew Jackson ordered the Cherokee removed from their homeland forever. They were sent from their beautiful Appalachians on a long trek to Indian Territory (now Oklahoma). Many died on that terrible journey called the Trail of Tears.

However, some hid in the mountains and became the Eastern Band of Cherokee. Others had married settlers and were called by English names. Among these was the Vann family; Emma Sansom was one of their descendants.

Emma was born in 1847 at Social Circle, Georgia, the youngest of thirteen children. Her mother, Lemila, was a niece of Chief Joseph Vann. Her father, Micajah Sansom, moved the family to a farm near the southern end of Lookout Mountain, on Black Creek about three miles from Gadsden, Alabama. Emma was only five.

Her father died a few years later. When the Civil War began, the only children left at home were Emma, her sister Jane, and brother Rufus, who enlisted in the Confederate army. Soon they would be caught in the violent clash of two armies.

THE LIGHTNING MULE BRIGADE

In April 1863, Union colonel Abel Streight was ordered to destroy a major railroad hub at Rome, Georgia, which carried supplies throughout Alabama and Georgia. Mostly mounted on mules (horses were scarce), his 1,700 men left Nashville and pushed through the mountains of north Alabama in what became known as the "Lightning Mule Brigade." Dogging their heels was Gen. Nathan Bedford Forrest and his cavalry of less than 500 men.

Streight's soldiers reached Black Creek, about two miles from the Sansoms' dogtrot house. It was a swollen, muddy stream, with steep clay banks that made it impossible to cross on mules and horses. Emma, who was nearly sixteen, watched from the porch. Years later, she told the story in this way:

> We were at home on the morning of May 2, 1863, when about eight or nine o clock a company of men wearing blue uniforms and riding mules and horses galloped past the house and went on towards the bridge. Pretty soon a great crowd of them came along, and some of them stopped at the gate and asked us to bring them some water. Sister and I each took a bucket of water, and gave it to them at the gate.

One of the Federal soldiers asked where their men folk were. Emma told him that their father had died, and six brothers were serving in the Confederate army.

"Do they think the South will whip?" he asked.

"They do," she said.

"What do you think about it?"

"I think God is on our side, and we will win," Emma told him.

"You do? Well, if you had seen us whip Colonel Roddey the other day and run him across the Tennessee

Emma Sansom. (Courtesy of Larry Johnson)

River, you would have thought God was on the side of the best artillery."

More soldiers dismounted and went into the house. They made themselves at home, searching for firearms and saddles. All they found was a lady's sidesaddle, from which one of them cut away the leather skirts.

A rough voice shouted from outside, "You men bring a chunk of fire with you, and get out of that house!" The officer then put guards around the house to protect the women from further invasion.

They soon learned what the burning coals were for. The men hurried to the bridge and set it afire. As the smoke rose, Emma's mother said, "Come with me, and we will pull our rails away, so they will not be destroyed."

When they reached the top of the hill, it was already too late. Some of their wooden fence rails were already piled on the bridge and burning brightly. The Yankees had formed a solid line to guard it on the other side. As the women turned back toward the house, another soldier approached at full speed. He was pursued by more men on horseback.

"Halt! Surrender!" they shouted.

The man stopped, threw up his hands, and handed over his gun. The

Emma Sansom's childhood home near Gadsden. (Courtesy of Larry Johnson)

officer to whom he surrendered said, "Ladies, do not be alarmed. I am General Forrest; I and my men will protect you from harm." Then he asked, "Where are the Yankees?"

Emma's mother said, "They have set the bridge on fire and are standing in line on the other side. If you go down that hill, they will kill the last one of you."

By this time, more of General Forrest's men had arrived, and shooting had commenced from both sides. Emma ran to the house, ahead of them all.

General Forrest dashed up to the gate and asked her, "Can you tell me where I can get across that creek?"

She told him that the closest bridge was two miles down the stream and not at all safe. However, she knew of a trail about two hundred yards above the bridge now burning, where the cows used to cross in low water. She believed that his men could cross there.

"If you will have my saddle put on a horse, I will show you the way," Emma told him.

"There is no time to saddle a horse; get up here behind me," said General Forrest. He rode close to the bank where she was standing, and she jumped up behind him.

Just as they started off, her mother appeared. "Emma, what do you mean?" she gasped.

"She is going to show me a ford where I can get my men over in time to catch those Yankees before they get to Rome," the general told her. "Don't be uneasy; I will bring her back safe."

They rode across a field through which ran a branch of the creek. Thick undergrowth shielded them from being seen by the Yankees at the bridge or on the other side. The branch emptied into the creek just above the ford.

When they got close to the creek, Emma said, "General Forrest, I think we had better get off the horse, as we are now where we may be seen."

She described what happened next:

> We both got down and crept through the bushes. The cannon and the other guns were firing fast by this time. I pointed out to him where to go into the water and out on the other bank, and then we went back towards the house. He asked me my name, and

asked me to give him a lock of my hair. The cannon-balls were screaming over us so loud that we were told to leave and hide in some place out of danger, which we did.

Soon all the firing stopped, and I started back home. On the way I met General Forrest again, and he told me that he had written a note for me and left it on the bureau. He asked me again for a lock of my hair. As we went into the house he said, "One of my bravest men has been killed, and he is laid out in the house. His name is Robert Turner. I want you to see that he is buried in some grave-yard near here."

He then told me good-bye and got on his horse. He and his men rode away, and left us all alone. My sister and I sat up all night watching over the dead soldier, who had lost his life fighting for our rights, in which we were overpowered but never conquered. General Forrest and his men endeared themselves to us forever.

VICTORY

The "lost ford" that Emma showed General Forrest was soon cleared and made passable. The cavalry went over, followed by heavy caissons hitched to double teams of horses that pulled them up the steep creek bank. The next day, General Forrest caught up with Colonel Streight's raiders just a few miles from Rome, Georgia, and forced them to surrender. General Forrest always gave credit to Emma for her bravery, the capture of the Union forces, and saving the railroad at Rome. This is the note he had left on her bureau:

Hed Quarters in Sadie
May 2 1863

My highest regardes to miss Emma Sansom for hir Gallant conduct while my posse was skirmishing with the Federals across Black Creek near Gadsden Allabama.

N. B. Forrest
Brig Genl Comding N. Ala

One week later, a Jacksonville newspaper reported Emma's story, calling her "A True Heroine." What captured the public's imagination about

> General Forrest was respected as a brilliant cavalry commander, but not for his spelling.

a simple farm girl's bravery? Perhaps it was her courage in the face of enemy fire, or possible consequences to her family if General Forrest had not been successful. Perhaps she represented the countless women and girls who gave food, water, first aid, encouragement, and directions to the soldiers who came to their doors.

The following year, the Alabama Assembly passed a resolution that Emma should be honored with a gold medal and a gift of 640 acres. She also married a soldier, Christopher Johnson. He was a neighbor who had been badly injured, leaving one leg four inches shorter than the other. While living in Alabama, they had a daughter named Mattie Forrest Johnson. After little Mattie died, they moved to Upshur County, Texas.

1916 United Confederate Veterans reunion, photographed at Emma's statue in Gadsden. (Courtesy of Michael Sharpton)

Christopher, who was several years older than Emma, died in 1887. At age forty, she was widowed with seven children, ages two to nineteen. The family farmed and remained close. In later years, Emma caught tuberculosis (then called "consumption").

In 1898, she was invited to the Grand Reunion of Confederate Veterans at Atlanta, Georgia. Seventy-five former Confederate soldiers escorted Emma on the train from Gadsden.

She lived until 1900, devoted to her church and growing family. A statue and school were built to honor her in Gadsden.

Modest Emma always felt that too much fuss had been made about her deed and rarely talked about the exciting day when General Forrest asked her how to cross the creek.

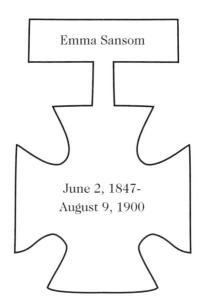

Emma Sansom

June 2, 1847-
August 9, 1900

Chapter 9

CHARLES W. READ

How does losing his father at a young age change a boy? Does it make him more responsible, self-reliant, angry, or undisciplined? When Charles W. Read's father left his family during the Gold Rush of 1849, the nine-year-old suddenly became "the man of the house." He was the oldest of five children and worked hard with his mother on their farm near the Yazoo River in Mississippi. When they received word the following year that their father had died in California, Maria Read sold the place and moved to the city.

Charlie, as his brothers called him, preferred life in Jackson, the state's busy capital. He had a lively mind and, as a teenager, wrote articles for a newspaper, *The Mississippian*. Several young employees joined together to start their own paper, called *Scraps of America*.

Charlie also became a member of a theater group. But he longed for more excitement and was fascinated by the sea. After running away to join a merchant ship in New Orleans, the boy was fetched home by his mother. She enrolled him in the Naval Academy at Annapolis, hoping that he would thrive under the discipline and new challenges.

Mother was partly right. The structure and sense of belonging to something greater than himself (the navy) were good for Charlie. While taking French, he was nicknamed *Savez* (pronounced "sahvay"), the only word he could pronounce correctly. Small, brown haired, wiry, and energetic, Charlie got demerits for fighting and was fiercely loyal to his friends. Though he had great common sense, Charles spent little time studying and graduated at the bottom of his class. But now he could go to sea!

GRADUATING CLASS OF 1860—25 MEMBERS—WARRANTED AS MIDSHIPMEN JUNE 15, 1860.

Order of general merit.	Names.	State.	Date of Admission.	Years.	Months.	Seamanship.	Naval Tactics.	Theory of Naval Gunnery.	Practical Gunnery.	Astronomy and Navigation.	Chemistry.	The Steam Engine.	Spanish.	Political Science.	Demerits for the year.
•1	M. S. Stuyvesant	Ohio	Sept. 23, 1856	16	2	13	2	6	2	1	1	1	2	1	18
•2	A. D. Wharton	Tenn.	Sept. 23, 1856	16	2	5	3	3	7	3	6	5	1	2	39
•3	J. D. Marvin	Ohio	Sept. 25, 1856	16	11	3	4	2	3	6	2	2	3	3	42
•4	John O'Kane	Ind.	Sept. 27, 1856	16	10	1	6	5	5	8	3	3	8	5	48
•5	S. P. Gillett	Ind.	Sept. 20, 1856	15	10	4	1	1	1	5	12	4	7	8	50
6	T. L. Swann	Md.	Dec. 8, 1856	15	4	7	8	7	11	9	9	7	6	4	8
7	T. L. Dornin	Va.	Sept. 22, 1856	16	2	8	13	8	19	4	16	23	12	6	123
8	S. D. Ames	R. I.	Sept. 23, 1856	16	2	2	5	12	4	2	14	12	13	17	116
9	J. C. Watson	Ky.	Sept. 29, 1856	14	1	18	20	10	10	7	5	6	4	7	68
10	J. L. Tayloe	Va.	Sept. 24, 1855	14	11	14	10	20	13	20	23	15	5	9	93
11	H. B. Robeson	Conn.	Sept. 25, 1856	14	2	9	14	9	9	12	13	19	18	12	40
12	A. R. McNair	Mo.	Sept. 23, 1856	17	0	10	21	4	6	21	7	8	21	18	42
13	W. H. Barton	Md.	Sept. 22, 1856	16	11	12	9	13	12	14	9	16	15	16	8
14	F. S. Brown	N. Y.	Sept. 24, 1856	16	6	6	7	11	15	11	21	14	14	15	76
15	H. De H. Manley	Penn.	Sept. 25, 1856	16	9	21	15	18	14	16	11	9	17	13	38
16	William Whitehead	Penn.	Sept. 23, 1856	16	3	16	22	19	8	13	4	10	9	10	69
17	E. A. Walker	Mass.	Sept. 24, 1855	14	9	20	17	23	23	23	8	18	11	19	30
18	W. S. Schley	Md.	Sept. 22, 1856	16	11	17	16	16	18	17	17	20	10	22	38
19	T. L. Harrison	Va.	Sept. 29, 1856	17	0	15	11	17	22	15	15	21	24	21	77
20	H. D. Hoole	Ala.	Sept. 22, 1856	15	8	24	24	14	17	19	20	11	22	11	0
21	S. D. Paddock	Ohio	Sept. 26, 1856	15	11	19	18	25	24	10	25	22	16	23	142
22	F. L. Hoge	Va.	Sept. 20, 1856	15	6	23	19	15	20	22	18	13	19	14	74
23	S. E. Casey, jr.	N. Y.	Sept. 25, 1856	16	0	11	12	22	16	18	19	17	9	25	40
24	Edmund G. Read	Va.	Sept. 25, 1855	16	1	22	23	24	21	24	24	24	23	20	69
25	Charles W. Read	Miss.	Sept. 29, 1856	16	4	25	25	21	25	25	22	25	25	24	88

The 1860 graduating class of the Naval Academy. (Courtesy of Lauderdale County Archives, Meridian, Mississippi)

USS POWHATAN

Charlie's first commission (assignment) was aboard the USS *Powhatan*. He was in the Gulf of Mexico when his home state of Mississippi seceded from the Union. After resigning from the U.S. Navy, he reported to the new Confederate capital in Montgomery, Alabama. He later described the mood of that time:

> From what I could learn, the people of the South were almost

unanimously in favor of the secession of the States, for the reason that they could see no other way of protecting their rights; but they hoped for peace and the friendship of the people of the North, and a great many hoped for a reunion, in which there would be no contentions, and in which the people of the South would be guaranteed equal rights with all the States.

I had been in Mississippi but a few days, when the country was aware that war had commenced, and that the stronghold of Fort Sumter, in Charleston harbor, had been compelled to surrender to the Southern forces. Soon news came that Lincoln had called for 75,000 men to march upon the States which had swung loose from the Federal Union. The youth of the South sprung to arms in obedience to the call of their President [Jefferson Davis], and everywhere the fife and drum were heard. It was, indeed, hard for me to keep from volunteering for the army, but I remembered that the South had but few sailors and would need them all on the water.

New Loyalties

Charlie met with President Davis, ready to do his part. On May 1, 1861, he reported for duty on the Confederate steamer *McRae* in New Orleans. He immediately liked the captain, Lt. Thomas Huger, and learned a good deal from him. All hands worked swiftly to prepare their ships for war, adding guns and iron plating as protection.

President Lincoln had just declared a blockade on all Confederate ports from Texas to Virginia. His goal was to choke the South by preventing trade with other countries. No cotton could be shipped out, nor weapons and supplies brought in. Everything was in short supply—coffee, medicine, clothing, shoes, and farm implements.

At first, the U.S. Navy had only ninety ships with which to patrol 3,500 miles of coastline. Most blockade runners (merchant ships) easily slipped through the loose network. But the navy soon grew to over three hundred ships. Flag Officer David Farragut's task was to control the country's great flowing highway—the Mississippi River.

Salt was so scarce that farmers dug up the floors of their smokehouses to recover salt from the meat drippings. Some newspapers stopped publishing for lack of paper.

His first step was to capture New Orleans, the Confederacy's largest port. Twenty boats steamed to the mouth of the river and pounded Fort St. Phillip and Fort Jackson with their cannon. Charlie's ship, the *McRae*, was hit broadside, and Lieutenant Huger was killed.

Charles Read. (Naval History and Heritage Command Photographic Division)

As next in command, Charlie quickly took charge. Guiding the damaged ship through floating wrecks and dense smoke, he got his wounded men to safety. When New Orleans surrendered, he was ordered to do the same. Damaged beyond repair, the *McRae* finally sank.

BATTLE OF THE IRONCLADS

Charlie's next duty was aboard the ironclad *Arkansas*. It was built of oak shielded with railroad iron, to resist bullets and cannon fire. Rust had turned its armor to a chocolate color, so it looked like a great, brown river monster plowing through the murky water.

By July 1862, over thirty Union ships gathered to attack Vicksburg, the last major Confederate stronghold on the Mississippi River. The *Arkansas*'s mission was to charge through Farragut's fleet, destroying as many ships as possible, and go on to Mobile. It was a daring plan. Over two hundred nervous young men waited below while Charlie watched on deck. Like Lieutenant Huger, he was calm and confident.

When the fighting began, the cannon's thunder could be heard ten miles away. Ships drifted through a blanket of smoke, so thick it was hard to tell friend from foe. The Union fleet surrounded the *Arkansas*, pounding its armor and killing many crewmen. Somehow the battered ironclad plowed on until it reached the protective guns of Vicksburg.

The *Arkansas* finally met its fate in Baton Rouge on August 6. Though some repairs had been made, it was still having engine trouble during a faceoff with the Union ironclad *Essex*. People watching from the levee cheered her on, but the *Arkansas* was a sitting duck. To save his crew, the captain sent them to shore, then blew up the ship.

COMMERCE RAIDERS

After serving at Port Hudson a short time, Charlie was ordered to Mobile. In response to the Union blockade, the Confederacy had bought two swift new ships to intercept Northern traders. Capt. John Maffitt of the *Florida*

Among the crowd was Sarah Morgan, a Baton Rouge girl who wrote about their disappointment in her diary. Her brother, Jimmy Morgan, served with Charlie on the *McRae*.

needed men who were fearless and loyal. His journal described Charlie this way: "*November 4.*—Lieutenant C. W. Read, the last lieutenant I personally applied for, joined; this officer acquired reputation for gunnery, coolness, and determination at the battle of New Orleans. When his commander, T. B. Huger, was fatally wounded he continued to gallantly fight."

Captain Maffitt believed that the raiders could help shorten the war: "When a man-of-war is sacrificed 'tis a national calamity, not individually felt, but when merchant ships are destroyed on the high seas individuality suffers, and the shoe then pinches in the right direction. All the merchants of New York and Boston who have by their splendid traders become princes in wealth and puffy with patriotic zeal for the subjugation of the South, will soon cry with a loud voice, peace, peace; we are becoming ruined."

FIRST COMMAND

Charlie was delighted with the prospect of getting out to sea again. He waited impatiently for a stormy night when the *Florida* could slip out through Union ships blocking Mobile Bay. Their daring escape was made on January 16, 1863.

In May, they captured the *Clarence,* a brig hauling coffee to Baltimore. Charlie asked Captain Maffitt for permission to take it on a raid up the East Coast. The captain agreed, giving Charlie his first real command.

Charlie and his "Prize Crew" of twenty-one sailed for Virginia, on a cruise that shook the confidence of the U.S. Navy. His orders were secret at first. The men wondered where they were going, but their solemn young captain confided in no one. Like soldiers and spies on the mainland, the raiders' tools were disguise, surprise, and a great deal of nerve.

The *Clarence* had only one Howitzer gun, a small cannon used for signaling. The men built several wooden "dummy" cannons, called Quaker guns. Dressed like a gunboat, the *Clarence* fooled several ships into surrender. At other times, the guns were hidden, the men changed to civilian clothes, and the flag was flown upside down at half-mast. This was the universal distress signal at sea. When another ship pulled alongside, it was boarded and captured for the Confederacy. Charlie then had three options:

1. Take everyone onboard as prisoners and burn the ship.
2. Require the other captain to sign a bond (pledge to pay the Confederate government) and then send them on their way.
3. Transfer his crew to the new ship.

The ship's fate depended on whose flag it flew and where it was going. Prisoners were a problem, since food and water were limited. None of Captain Read's prisoners was killed. Instead they were each allowed to bring one bag of personal items, and the men were locked below deck. Charlie then found creative ways to release the hundreds of prisoners who fell into his hands. It might be putting them on a neutral ship or another captured vessel or sending them ashore in a rowboat.

Northern newspapers accused the Confederate raiders of piracy, and Secretary of the Navy Gideon Welles called them "wolves." But to Southerners suffering from the blockade, they quickly became heroes. Crewmen who had questioned Charlie's judgment at first were now proud to be serving under the daring young captain.

A Quaker gun mounted on a bluff at Port Hudson. (Library of Congress)

The East Coast was on alert as U.S. naval boats patrolled its waters. Charlie kept them guessing by switching to two different ships, the swift *Tacony* and the *Archer*. His final prize was the *Caleb Cushing*. After a daring night raid into the harbor at Portland, Maine, circumstances turned against him. The *Caleb Cushing* got stuck in shallow mud and had to be towed from the harbor, losing precious time. At dawn, the alert was sounded when U.S. crewmen on shore leave realized that their ship was missing!

The *Caleb Cushing* sailed toward the open sea as fishing villages awoke. Citizens in every kind of vessel took up the chase. Before the *Caleb Cushing* could escape, the wind died down. A Union vessel opened fire. Charlie and his crew frantically searched for ammunition but didn't know where it was hidden. They never found it and had to abandon the smoking ship. When the Union vessel approached their rowboats, a grim but dignified Charlie climbed aboard. Looking like a boy in his oversized peacoat, the weary young captain surrendered. From June 6 to 27, Charlie and his crew had captured twenty-one ships—three on the same day. Imagine the enemy's surprise to learn that the Sea Wolf of the Confederacy was only twenty-three years old!

The Tacony *burning enemy vessels.* (*Harper's Weekly*, Library of Congress)

Destruction of the Caleb Cushing. (*Harper's Weekly*, Library of Congress)

The Last Run

Charlie was imprisoned at Fort Warren in Boston Harbor. He escaped three times, only to be caught outside. In the last attempt, he chipped away mortar from inside a chimney and climbed out. However, while he was hiding under a canvas, his leg was speared with a bayonet; the injury troubled him for years.

When finally released in a prisoner exchange, Charlie was given command of the CSS *William Webb*. To run the blockade, it was disguised as a Union vessel taking cotton down the Red River and the Mississippi and on to sell in Cuba.

The *Webb* set off on April 16, 1865. Along the way, Charlie learned that General Lee had surrendered on April 9, and President Lincoln had died on the morning of April 15. He continued downriver, still hoping to help the Confederacy. The *Webb* almost made it to the Gulf of Mexico when a warship blocked its path. Charlie burned his boat before surrendering to the Union captain, a former classmate at Annapolis.

AFTER THE WAR

In 1867, Charlie married Rosaltha Hall, whom he had met before the war. She died of yellow fever in 1878, leaving him with three young children. In 1884, he married again and had another daughter.

Always at home on the water, Charlie became a Mississippi riverboat pilot and harbormaster of New Orleans. He died of pneumonia at age forty-nine. As a classmate from Annapolis said, "America never produced a naval officer more worthy of a place in history."

In 1879, Lt. Charles W. Read was awarded the Confederate Medal of Honor.

Charles W. Read

May 12, 1840-
January 25, 1890

Chapter 10

WILLIAM H. YOPP

Bill Yopp was born in 1845 on Whitehall plantation, one of the largest in Laurens County, Georgia. Both of his parents worked for Jeremiah Yopp and were given the family name as their own. They went to church services every week. Though most slaves were not taught to read and write, they could recite many Bible passages.

Little Bill was seven when he was given to Thomas Yopp, one of the master's sons. Bill said later that he was like "Mary's Little Lamb," since where Thomas went, he was sure to go. Thomas was older, about twenty-four, and loved to hunt and fish. Bill was always there, holding the horses and learning how to hunt quail and catch trout. The boys grew close as Bill followed Thomas everywhere—even off to war.

When the war began, Thomas joined the Blackshear Guards, as an officer in Company H of the Fourteenth Georgia Infantry. Fifteen-year-old Bill wanted to go with him and was allowed to enlist as a private. He worked as Thomas's body servant, a personal attendant who guarded his belongings and took care of his needs.

Bill was pleasant, hardworking, and well liked in his regiment. The men taught him how to read and write and took care of him when he was sick. According to Bill, no one ever said an unkind word to him. When not looking after Thomas, he shined shoes and did other chores for the men. Whatever the task, he always

> Thousands of African Americans, slave and free, served in the Confederate army, as soldiers, musicians, teamsters, and body servants.

asked for a dime in payment. He often had more money than anyone in Company H! Soon the men gave him a nickname—"Ten Cent Bill." It stayed with him for the rest of his life.

Once, when Thomas was away on furlough, Bill joined the others in foraging for whatever food was available. Some soldiers politely asked citizens if they had food to spare, but many just helped themselves. On one occasion, a farmer let the soldiers pick apples from his orchard while his wife cooked the men a meal. After Thomas returned, Bill went foraging again and brought back ears of corn to roast. Thomas called it stealing and ordered him not to go again.

DRUM CORPS

Company H joined the Army of Northern Virginia, with Thomas as captain of the regiment. Bill was made a drummer. Before walkie-talkies and radios, musicians played an important role in keeping soldiers organized. Music could lift the men's spirits and inspire them to action, just as it does today.

Drummers or buglers started the day with reveille at five o'clock, to get the men out of bed and to breakfast. They also announced roll call and attention and set the cadence for marching. In battle, they drummed out signals to assemble, advance, and retreat.

When regiments were camped for long periods of time, musicians formed bands to play for dress parades and concerts. Very often, the music could be heard in the enemy camp. Sometimes there was a "battle of the bands" between opposing sides, using songs such as "Dixie" (south) and "Battle Hymn of the Republic" (north). At special moments, bands in enemy camps might join to play the same tune, such as "Home Sweet Home."

Musicians also helped tend the wounded. They served as medics, carried stretchers, helped surgeons in the field hospital, and buried the dead.

About a dozen books of military band music have survived. A concert might have included patriotic tunes, sentimental ballads, a polka, or a waltz.

Drum Corps, Ninety-Third New York Infantry. (Library of Congress)

Though musicians carried no weapons, they were killed in battle, too. Drummers marched at the front of a battle line, an especially dangerous place to be. Bill never liked that part of his duty.

Though Bill often found himself between battle lines and could have

> It was said that Bill rescued dying and wounded soldiers, both Confederate and Union, from the battlefield and was called "the Dark Angel."

escaped his slavery by going to the Union side, he never did. He said, "I had no inclination to go to the Union side, as I did not know the Union soldiers and the Confederate soldiers I did know, and I believed then as now, tried and true friends are better than friends you do not know."

COMPANY H

Thomas was wounded in the shoulder at the Battle of Seven Pines. Bill was with him at the field hospital, the huge military hospital at Richmond, and then home for his recuperation. They returned in time for the Battle of Fredericksburg in December 1862. A shell burst above

Thomas, knocking him unconscious. Bill cared for the captain until he was healed. By then, the faithful servant was suffering from exhaustion and homesickness. Thomas sent him home for a rest. He soon returned and witnessed the terrible battles at Gettysburg and Chancellorsville.

In the summer of 1863, Thomas went home for several months. He then joined the Confederate Navy; this time Bill was not allowed to follow. In May 1865, after Lee's surrender, Bill learned that Thomas was back onshore. Going to meet his friend, he saw the wagon train carrying Pres. Jefferson Davis as he tried to leave the Confederacy.

SEEING THE WORLD

Times were hard for everyone after the war. General Sherman's troops had burned and plundered much of Georgia. Plantation owners told their former slaves that they were free to do as they pleased. Those who stayed on the farm could rent a piece of land in exchange for a percentage of their crop.

Some, especially the older people and those who had been well treated, chose to stay. At least they would have food and shelter in a devastated country. Others left to seek their fortune or find family members from whom they had been separated by slavery.

Bill tried sharecropping until 1870. Then he moved to Macon and worked as a bellboy at the Brown House. There he met some of Georgia's "rich and famous." When Mr. Brown, the old gentleman who owned the hotel, went home to Connecticut, he asked Bill to travel with him. Along the way,

Bill Yopp. (Courtesy of Laurens County Historical Society, Dublin, Georgia)

they visited New York City, where Bill loved the excitement.

Bill returned to Georgia in 1873 and worked as a porter on the Charleston and Savannah Railroad. Then he came down with yellow fever, lost fifty pounds, and went home to Macon to recover. While there, he was able to spend time with Thomas, hunting and fishing as they had in the old days.

FINDING THOMAS

As time passed, the little boy from Georgia grew up to tell stories about Europe, Hawaii, and typhoons in the Indian Ocean. He also worked in the private car of a railroad superintendent. When the train stopped in Atlanta, Bill took his free day to visit the Confederate Veterans Home. There he found his old friend, Thomas Yopp, who was in his eighties. He was alone, and his land now belonged to someone else. It was a sad ending for the former soldiers whose families, if they had one, were unable to care for them.

Bill decided to bring them some cheer. "Foraging" from his paycheck, he

Bill Yopp and Thomas Yopp. (Courtesy of Laurens County Historical Society, Dublin, Georgia)

Bill's résumé included:
- waiter in a hotel in Albany, New York
- serving a family in California
- visiting London, Paris, Berlin, and Brussels
- cooking for a ship's captain

bought treats and "played Santa" for Thomas and other men who could not afford luxuries on their small pensions. Before long, Bill's actions made the newspaper in their hometown. He asked the *Macon Daily Telegraph* to promote a Christmas fund for the veterans, which they did for three years. His biography, *Ten Cent Bill,* was published as a fundraiser. Contributions came from all over the state.

Also in the news was the fighting in Europe, as World War I raged on. Bill found work nearby and continued his fundraising for the Veterans Home. In 1919, he was invited by the governor to speak to Georgia's legislators about money for the veterans. They voted to send $500 to the Veterans Home each Christmas.

Thomas died in 1920, at age ninety-two, with Bill by his side. Thomas had lost a great deal in his life but kept his oldest friend. Bill spoke at the funeral service. He was then offered Thomas's room at the Veterans Home and awarded a medal of appreciation by the veterans. Bill spent his remaining years there and became the only African American buried in the Confederate Cemetery in Marietta, Georgia.

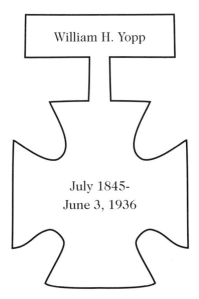

William H. Yopp

July 1845-
June 3, 1936

Chapter 11

DANIEL JACKSON COLLINS

When the Spanish landed in Florida in the 1500s, they were searching for gold. Not finding it, they stayed anyway, bringing a new language, culture, and diseases to the native peoples. They also brought horses, pigs, and cattle. Their hardy cows, called Andalusians, adapted to the New World and multiplied. Soon their descendants were scattered across Florida's palmetto prairie and marshland.

In 1844, Enoch and Fatima Collins came from Georgia to homestead in central Florida. They rounded up the wild-ranging cattle and put on their mark, or brand. Unlike Texas cowboys, who used ropes for herding, Florida cowmen cracked braided-leather whips that were ten to twelve feet long. They became known as "crackers," a nickname that is still used today.

The Collinses built a cabin and filled it with fourteen children. Daniel was the first of the family to be born in Florida. That was in 1845, the year Florida became a state. For both Daniel and the newborn state, life would be filled with turmoil.

Daniel's mother died a year later. Enoch married Elizabeth and they had six children. Since health care was poor, and many people did not live to be grandparents, she died as well. Enoch married again and had nine more children, for a total of twenty-nine! Even during a time when people raised large families, this was amazing.

Daniel grew up working the livestock and learning from his older brothers. The new state was only sixteen years old when it seceded from the Union. Since the preferred military age was eighteen to thirty-five,

The 1860 census shows that, out of 77,746 whites living in the new state, only 5,152 owned slaves.

Florida contributed more than fifteen thousand troops to the Confederacy. About five thousand Floridians died in the war.

Daniel was too young to volunteer. Four of his older brothers joined the Fourth Florida Infantry and went North to assist the Army of Tennessee. Brothers William and Samuel later joined other units.

The soldiers from Florida fought in terrible battles across the South. They were at Stones River in Murfreesboro, Chickamauga, Chattanooga, Jackson, Missionary Ridge, and in North Carolina. The Fourth Infantry was organized with 983 men. By December 1863, only 198 were left for roll call.

The Collins brothers who joined the Fourth Infantry were scattered as the war took its toll:

- Enoch, Jr., was wounded in September 1863 and spent months in a hospital.
- James was captured at the Battle of Missionary Ridge on November 25, 1863. He was sent to prison camp at Rock Island, Illinois, where he stayed until the war ended.
- Jesse, who joined at age eighteen, was wounded in both arms and worked as a nurse. He was promoted to third lieutenant before his capture at Decatur, Georgia in July 1864. He spent almost a year at Johnson's Island prison in Ohio.
- John was thirty when the war began. He became the company cook and was one of sixty volunteers from the Fourth Florida to be sent home. Their mission was to protect the cows!

Cow Cavalry

In 1862, it was estimated that over 650,000 "cracker cows" roamed the palmetto prairie and grasslands of Florida. After the Mississippi River fell under Union control in 1863, Texas cattle were no longer available to the Confederacy. The blockade prevented many supplies from entering

"Support the Soldiers" flyer.
(Courtesy of the Tampa Tribune)

One of Florida's major contributions to the Confederacy was livestock. Another was salt, which was necessary to preserve meat. Salt-making along Florida's gulf coast involved boiling seawater in large kettles or containers to evaporate the water and collect the salt. In 1863, the main Florida salt works produced more than 7,500 bushels per day.

Southern harbors. The Confederate Army desperately needed food for its soldiers, and prisoners in Union camps such as Andersonville were starving. At one point, prison guards were sent to assist the drovers, but fighting in Georgia prevented them from bringing back the needed beef. The average Confederate soldier only had meat in his rations about twice a week.

Florida ranchers had been herding their cattle to the railroad depots in Georgia, where they were distributed to the army. Union raids were choking this supply line. Gangs of deserters also roamed the countryside, burning farms and stealing whatever they could find. Protecting the cattle had become dangerous business.

Capt. James McKay of Tampa wrote to the Confederate War Department, saying, "The government is blinded to their interest in leaving this country [undefended] as they do." At his suggestion, the First Florida Special Cavalry Battalion was formed—the Cow Cavalry. The red-and-white speckled cows had become quite a treasure! When the Army of Tennessee asked for volunteers, sixty men from the Fourth Florida Infantry agreed to return home with Maj. Charles Munnerlyn. He needed men who could work cattle and defend themselves.

Once in Florida, Capt. John T. Lesley began recruiting troops from the Tampa Bay area. He called for volunteers, from men too old and boys too young for the draft. Ranchers, who had been exempt from military service, now joined to protect their herds.

The Cow Cavalry grew to nine companies totaling around nine hundred men. Five Collins boys were on the roster of Company B, who called themselves "The Sandpipers": Daniel, Enoch, Jr., Hardy, John, and William. Daniel was eighteen by now. It's possible that his younger brother Perry also served as a courier.

Company B's headquarters was in Hillsborough County. Cattle could only be driven during seasons when grass was available—from April till first frost. During the winter, the company patrolled the Tampa Bay coastline, rounded up deserters, guarded blockade runners, and fought Federal forces stationed in Jacksonville and St. Augustine. This helped bring order to the area, and citizens began returning to their homes.

When spring came, the Cow Cavalry organized drovers to round up and drive the cattle. They came from everywhere. The Cow Cavalry guarded a supply line over three hundred miles long. Each week, herds of about five hundred cattle were moved in relays, from central Florida to Savannah, Georgia and Charleston, South Carolina. The company had to deal with not only thieves and enemy soldiers but also mosquitoes, snakes, heat, and other dangers lurking in the palmetto prairie.

The area around Lake Okeechobee was well known for its herds, and the village of Orlando was an important watering hole at the time.

Company B had several skirmishes with Federal troops, including one in which Captain Lesley was shot in the left arm. The doctor wanted to amputate it, but Captain Lesley refused. Instead, he ordered one of the Collins boys and another soldier to stand guard in case he lost consciousness. Unless the arm "turned blue," no doctor was to remove it! The guards obeyed, and the arm was saved, though stuck in one position.

The Cow Cavalry pushed on as the Confederacy struggled through the last year of the war. No one knows how many soldiers, and Federal prisoners, survived because of their efforts. However, as the herding season began in April 1865, word reached Florida that Robert E. Lee had surrendered in Virginia. The last herd of 500 cattle was delivered that week.

Very few Southern families received all their loved ones back safely. The Collins family was an exception. Though they had been scattered, starved, wounded, and imprisoned, all eight of the Collins boys came home!

Two years later, Daniel married Sarah Platt and continued to work his land. In time, the hardy cracker cows were replaced with larger breeds to supply a modern market. Daniel and Sarah had nine children, whose descendants can still be heard cracking their whips at the county fair!

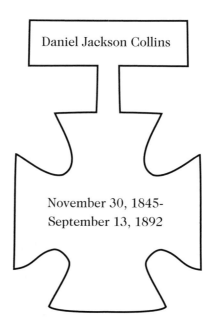

Daniel Jackson Collins

November 30, 1845-
September 13, 1892

Chapter 12

SARAH MORGAN

The year 1861 was a terrible one for young Sarah Morgan. On January 26, her home state of Louisiana seceded from the Union. In April, her beloved brother Harry was killed in a duel, and the nation went to war. Her father, a respected judge, died that autumn.

Sarah was nineteen when the war started. Though born in New Orleans, she had moved at age eight to Baton Rouge, the state capital. Her home was three blocks from the Mississippi River, within sight of the beautiful State House. There was a military arsenal, which had been filled with the sounds of soldiers drilling before the war began. Then they were called to other parts of the country.

Sarah's father had opposed secession, but he supported his three sons who joined the Confederacy. Gibbes and George fought in the East, while young Jimmy joined the navy. Another son, a judge in New Orleans, sided with the Union.

The war reached Baton Rouge in April 1862. Gunboats battled for control of New Orleans, the South's largest port. The Federal fleet

Sarah Morgan.

Louisiana's castle-like State House was built in the 1840s on land once owned by Sarah's family. The interior was burned in December 1862 while occupied by Federal troops.

State House after it burned while occupied by Federal troops. (Courtesy of LSU Libraries Special Collections)

under Adm. David Farragut finally broke through and pushed upriver. Their goal was to control the great, muddy Mississippi.

Farragut's men steamed through its twists and turns, between lazy bayous and grassy levees that protected cane fields and stately plantation homes. The women, children, and few men left in Baton Rouge grew more nervous with each new report. Sarah wrote in her diary:

April 26, 1862

There is no word in the English language which can express the state in which we are all now, and have been for the last three days. Day before yesterday news came early in the morning of three of the enemy's boats passing the forts, and then the excitement commenced.

Sarah's sister Lilly hurried to pack up her five children in case they were forced to evacuate. The men still in town, including Lilly's husband, decided to burn the cotton. A flatboat was piled with huge bales, set ablaze, and floated down the river in a sheet of living flame. Drifting smoke stung Sarah's blue eyes. It was a year's worth of work and a terrible waste. But if the owners could not sell it, she realized, neither should the Yankees. She went home to pack.

If the house had to burn, I had to make up my mind to run. So my treasure bag being tied around my waist as a bustle, a sack on

Gunboats at Baton Rouge. (Library of Congress)

my arm with a few necessary trifles . . . I stood ready for instant flight. My papers I piled on the bed, ready to burn, with matches lying on them.

OCCUPATION

The waiting continued for two weeks as the citizens of Baton Rouge held their breath. On May 9, a Federal gunboat landed, demanding their surrender. Though the citizens were defenseless, the mayor refused. Soldiers replaced the city's Stars and Bars flag with the Stars and Stripes and threatened to shell the town if it was disturbed. In defiance, Sarah joined other ladies in wearing small Confederate flags made from ribbon.

At church that Sunday, she was shocked when a group of Federal officers walked into the service. Watching the men who sat in front of her, Sarah realized they must belong to the same faith as she did. They had brought the *Book of Common Prayer* and knew exactly what to do. How could these men, who worshipped the same God and in the same manner, be her enemy?

As Sarah turned to sit down, the full hoops under her skirt bumped her prayer book, knocking it into the seat in front—right onto a soldier's hat! She panicked inside, wondering if anyone saw. Girls sometimes did such things to get a man's attention. What if someone thought she was *flirting* with the enemy? When the service ended, Sarah flew out the door, leaving her book behind.

ATTACK!

May 17, 1862

One of these days when we are at peace, and all quietly settled in some corner of this wide world without anything particularly exciting to alarm us every few moments . . . we will wonder how we could await each day and hour with such anxiety . . . and if it were really possible that half the time as we lay down to sleep, we did not know that we might be homeless and beggars in the morning. It will look unreal then; we will say it was imagination; but it is bitterly true now.

Another tense week passed. Baton Rouge felt the effects of the blockade as merchants ran out of everything. Since Sarah's shoes were worn beyond repair, she went shopping. In every store, it was the same story—shoes, cloth, pins, tools, and canned goods were all in short supply. There were no ladies' shoes in town that fit her tiny feet. She finally settled for a pair of boys' shoes made from the skin of a crocodile.

The family was going about their routine one morning when the boom of cannon rattled the windows! Sarah's mother screamed, and Lilly hysterically gathered her children. Tiche, a servant who was bathing the baby, ran out with her wrapped in a towel.

Trying to stay calm, Sarah grabbed her

Southern women became masters of substitution:
- Confederate flour = cornmeal
- Coffee = barley, corn, okra, or peanuts
- Bridle = rope halter
- Silver = tin cup or spoon
- Pins = thorns

bonnet, treasure bag, and birdcage containing her pet bird Jimmy, named for her brother. Panicked women and screaming children crowded the streets, running away from the river and out of the gunboat's range. Sarah realized she could not carry Jimmy's heavy cage very far. With tears in her eyes, she set him free.

BETWEEN TWO FIRES

After the stampede to the countryside, some of the family returned home. The house had been plundered by soldiers but was not damaged. Southern guerrilla fighters gathered in nearby woods, waiting for Confederate general Breckenridge and his troops to arrive. They threatened to burn the city rather than let the Yankees keep it.

Rumors flew and alarms continued. Having used all the pages in her diary, Sarah was desperate for something to write in, a lightning rod for her mental thunder. She settled for her father's old ledgers.

Monday, June 16, 1862
     There is no use trying to break off journalizing in "these trying times." It has become a necessity to me. I get nervous and unhappy thinking of the sad condition of the country, and of the misery in store for us; get desperate to think I am fit for nothing in the world, could not earn my daily bread even. Just before I reach the lowest ebb, I dash off half a dozen lines, sing "Better days are coming," and Presto! am myself again.

Unlike most girls her age, Sarah was not overly concerned with finding a husband. Friends said her standards were too high, but she was determined to wait for her "perfect man." However, both she and her sister Miriam worried about how to support themselves. If the war was lost, Confederate money would be worthless, and the family jewelry would not last long.

Her only work experience was teaching Lilly's children and leading Bible classes for the servants. Except for ten months of formal schooling, her education had been at home. There was no higher education for girls available to her, though she longed for it. But her father had a wonderful library, and Sarah loved to read. She marveled at the laws of arithmetic and science and studied to be fluent in French.

A new Federal commander, Gen. Thomas Williams, soon arrived to maintain order. Believing that the guerrillas would not burn Baton Rouge with women and children there, he refused to let them leave without permission. Miriam met with the general to ask for a pass. She was surprised when he thoughtfully offered an escort and also a guard for their house. Miriam suspected it was because their oldest sister was married to a Federal officer serving in California. The general seemed to know everything about their family.

Though Miriam refused the help, a Colonel McMillan showed up on their doorstep anyway. Sarah hesitated to let him in, wondering what the neighbors would say. He offered to guard their home against roaming soldiers, but Sarah's mother sent him away. Then a barrel of flour was delivered. Sarah's mother struggled over whether to accept or return it. In the end she kept the flour and made Sarah write a thank-you note.

They heard later that Colonel McMillan had been shot. Sarah and Miriam argued about whether to return the colonel's kindness and help him. Should they risk being labeled as traitors, or stay home and do nothing? As a compromise, their mother agreed to send Tiche with bandages and food. Sarah searched for the linen, thinking:

> Our three brothers may be sick or wounded at this minute. What I do for this man, God will send someone to do for them. Let our "friends" burn our home for it. I would be proud to sacrifice myself for God and religion. Mob shall never govern my opinions, or tell me how much I may be allowed to do. I will do what Conscience alone dictates.

BATTLE OF BATON ROUGE

Tensions were great that summer, as Baton Rouge grew crowded with Federal soldiers wounded in the fighting up at Vicksburg. There were far too many for the medical staff to look after, and several died each day. Sarah fretted, but her mother would not consent for her daughters to help, since nursing was not considered proper work for young unmarried ladies. Instead, they scraped linen for bandages.

On August 2, word came to evacuate. General Breckenridge and his troops were only a few miles away. The Morgan ladies crossed the Mississippi by ferry, then made their way to Linwood, a plantation owned by in-laws. The Battle of Baton Rouge started three days later.

Sarah watched from the levee as the Confederate ironclad *Arkansas* chugged down the river to support General Breckenridge. The homely river monster, which had caused such panic at Vicksburg, was damaged and struggled to stay on course. Finally, the engine stopped and the boat drifted to shore. Since the Union ironclad *Essex* was coming to meet the *Arkansas,* the *Arkansas*'s captain ordered the crew off. They would blow the boat up rather than allow the Yankees to capture it.

As the *Arkansas*'s tired, dirty crew reached the shore, Sarah recognized Lt. Charles Read, a friend of her brother Jimmy. She had met him when the two young men served together on the *McRae.* Now she rushed down the twenty-foot levee to greet him. Charles blushed as he shook her hand. Looking him over, Sarah understood why. Instead of a crisp lieutenant's uniform, he was dressed in rough sailor's pants, a grimy threadbare shirt, boots, and an old straw hat.

However, clothes seemed unimportant as they sadly watched the

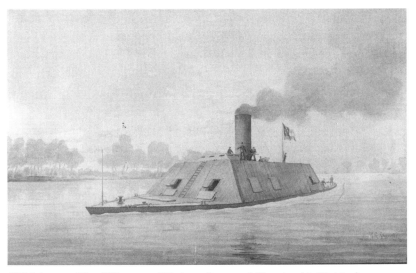

CSS Arkansas. (Naval History and Heritage Command Photographic Division)

Sarah's brother James (Jimmy) Morgan wrote a book about his adventures at sea, *Recollections of a Rebel Reefer*. Charles Read became known as the Sea Wolf of the Confederacy.

Arkansas burn. The Union *Essex* had arrived, then turned around to watch. They later claimed a great victory, though they had inflicted no damage to the *Arkansas*.

Cannon thunder rolled, and fire engulfed the Baton Rouge skyline. Would the Morgan home survive?

It was weeks before Sarah knew the fate of her home. When the armies left, she rode back through a burned Yankee camp, mounds of fresh graves, and the terrible stench of death. But her home was still standing!

Sarah and her brother-in-law wandered through the house. It was in ruin. Furniture had been stolen or destroyed, mirrors smashed, and her dresses ripped with a bayonet. The bright spot in it all was when a neighbor brought her little bird Jimmy, who had never left home.

LINWOOD

Sarah and Miriam spent several months at Linwood. The plantation was five miles from Port Hudson, a Confederate stronghold on the river. Officers came often for a home-cooked meal and good company. To impress the young ladies, they invited them to a dress parade at the fort. Sarah was enjoying the October day when a rifle shot spooked the horse pulling her carriage. He bolted and the carriage turned over, sending her in a somersault through the air. Sharp pains pierced her back after her hard landing, and she could not walk.

Back at Linwood, doctors came and went, all with the latest forms of medical torture. Sarah tried to be cheerful but poured frustration into her diary:

> First comes a doctor with a butchering apparatus who cups and bleeds me unmercifully, says I'll walk ten days after, and exit. . . .
> Enter another. Croton oil and strychnine pills. That'll set me up in two weeks, and exit. . . .
> Enter a third. Tells of the probability of a splinter of bone knocked off my left hip, the possibility of paralysis in the leg, and necessity for the most violent counter irritants . . .

Enter the fourth. Inhuman butcher! Wonder they did not kill you! Take three drops a day out of this tiny bottle, and presto! In two weeks you are walking! . . .

A fifth says, "Your case is hopeless."

The following May, Port Hudson was attacked. The girls watched and listened from a bedroom window, wondering which of their friends might be wounded or dead. Since Sarah was still in poor health, her mother decided it was time to find better medical care—even if it meant leaving the Confederacy. With heavy hearts they said farewell to Linwood and made the long, difficult journey to New Orleans. Sarah's oldest brother, Philip, was there to meet them.

The Siege of Port Hudson lasted forty-eight days, one of the longest in U.S. history. Though the men ran out of food and were forced to eat rats, they did not surrender until Vicksburg fell.

Sunday, April 26, New Orleans

I am getting well! Bless the Lord O my soul! On Thursday, a day to be marked with a white stone in my memory, for the first time since the eleventh of November, I discarded my nightgown, put on a dress and—walked to breakfast!

THE WAR ENDS

Gibbes and George never returned home. Jimmy married and traveled the world, taking Sarah and their mother along. Their new home was in South Carolina, where Sarah found her "perfect man." Frank Dawson was an Englishman who had fought for the Confederacy. He also published a Charleston newspaper and invited Sarah to write articles from a female viewpoint. It was unusual for a woman to write editorials, but she jumped at the chance to make a living.

Frank and Sarah married and raised two children. After his death, she moved to Paris with their son, Warrington. There she wrote *Les*

Aventures de Jeannot Lapin, a French version of the Brer Rabbit tales for children. Sarah died in France at age sixty-seven. She left six precious diaries to her son, who had begged her not to burn them. They were published in 1913. She once wrote:

I wonder why I could never keep a respectable diary. I have tried to look back here and there, to find one redeeming touch, one description as interesting or amusing as the original, but have been forced to relinquish the search from sheer disgust. I am strongly tempted to throw it in the fire every time I look at it. There is but one thing that withholds me; and that is the fact of its being the work of my sick hours when pen and ink proved my best friends. One should not forget tried friends.

Then I'll keep this as a souvenir of my dark days—those days when Hope threatened to unfold her wings and leave me a cripple on this fair earth, and I struggled boldly to make the world believe she had not gone yet, and did not mean to.

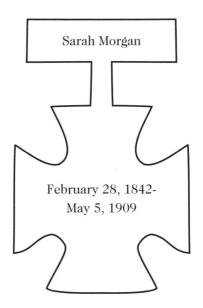

Sarah Morgan

February 28, 1842-
May 5, 1909

Glossary

aeronaut—someone who flies in a blimp or hot-air balloon.

amputate—to surgically remove a part of the body.

barrel staves—long wooden slats used to make barrels.

bayonet—metal blade attached to the end of a musket and used in close combat.

blockade—effort by the North to keep ships from entering or leaving Southern ports.

blockade runner—fast, light ship used for evading the naval blockade of a port.

body servant—slave who accompanied his master to war; he might cook, wash clothes, and take care of his horse.

Border States—Maryland, Delaware, Kentucky, and Missouri; although they did not officially join the Confederacy, many of their citizens supported the South.

cavalry—branch of the military mounted on horseback.

courier—soldier who carried mail and messages.

emancipation—freedom from slavery.

evacuate—to leave a dangerous place, such as a war zone.

foraging—expedition to find food and water.

furlough—leave from duty, granted by a superior officer.

guerrillas—small groups of civilians using military tactics to harass a larger army.

ironclad—steam-propelled warship fitted with plates of iron armor.

levee—natural or manmade earthen embankment along a river that controls its overflow.

Minié ball—bullet invented by a Frenchman that expanded when fired.

picket—person stationed as a guard, one of the most hazardous duties.

prosthetic—artificial body part.

Quaker guns—logs cut and painted to resemble cannon, to fool the enemy.

reconnaissance—exploring an area to gather information about enemy forces.

reveille—military signal to get up in the morning.

scouts—young soldiers who gathered information about roads, bridges, and troop movements, while in uniform.

secession—Southern states, feeling persecuted by the North, voted to separate from the Union; they felt this was perfectly legal, but Unionists saw it as rebellion.

sharecropper—tenant farmer who gives a share of his crops to the landlord as rent.

skirmish—fight between small groups of troops.

surveillance—observation of a person or group.

wigwag flag—flag on a long pole used to signal over a distance.

windlass—device using a rope or cable wrapped around a revolving drum to lift things such as a ship's anchor.

Bibliography

"An Address by A. W. Taft, before Camp Sumter C. V." *Charleston Sunday News*, May 1, 1897.

Barrow, Charles, J. Segars, and R. Rosenburg. *Forgotten Confederates: An Anthology about Black Southerners*. Mechanicsville, PA: Stackpole Books, 1997.

The Battle of Stones River. Washington, DC: National Park Service, U.S. Department of the Interior.

Blackburn, J. K. P. "Reminiscences of Terry's Rangers." *Southwestern Historical Quarterly* 22 (October 1918): 143-79.

Bolsterli, Margaret J. *A Remembrance of Eden: Harriet Bailey Bullock Daniel's Memories of a Frontier Plantation in Arkansas, 1849-1872*. University of Arkansas Press, 1993.

Boltz, Martha M. "James Edward Hanger: Civil War amputee creates jointed artificial leg." *Washington Times*, June 8, 2011.

Brown, Dee. "War on Horseback." *The National Historical Society's The Image of War 1861-1865*. Vol. 4, *Fighting For Time*. Garden City, NY: Doubleday, 1983.

Bruce, Philip A. *Brave Deeds of Confederate Soldiers*. Philadelphia: George W. Jacobs, 1916.

Campbell, R. Thomas. "Saga of the CSS *Webb*." *Confederate Veteran* (July-August 1994).

Charles W. Read Papers, Collection No. 424. Greenville, NC: J. Y. Joyner Library, East Carolina University.

"Charlie William Read." *Dictionary of American Biography*. 1935.

Clemmer, Gregg S. *Valor in Gray: The Recipients of the Confederate Medal of Honor*. Staunton, VA: Hearthside, 1998.

Company B, 1st Battalion Florida Special Cavalry, CSA. Muster roll.

Cummins, Edmund H. "The Signal Corps in the Confederate States Army." *Southern Historical Society Papers* 16 (1888).

Cunningham, H. H. *Doctors in Gray: The Confederate Medical Service.* Baton Rouge: LSU Press, 1960.

Cutrer, Thomas W. "8th Texas Cavalry: Terry's Texas Rangers." *Handbook of Texas Online.* Texas State Historical Association.

Dawson, Sarah Morgan. *A Confederate Girl's Diary.* Edited by Warrington Dawson. New York: Houghton Mifflin, 1913.

"Died Attended by Ex-Slave." *New York Times,* January 25, 1920.

"Dr. Simon Baruch, Long Ill, Dies at 80." *New York Times,* June 4, 1921.

Driver, Robert J. *14th Virginia Calvary.* Virginia Regimental History Series.

Dyer, Gustavus W., and John T. Moore, eds. *The Tennessee Civil War Veterans Questionnaires.* Vol. 5. Easley, SC: Southern Historical, 1985.

East, Charles. *Sarah Morgan: The Civil War Diary of a Southern Woman.* New York: Simon and Schuster, 1991.

1860. Cherokee, AL: Census Place, Division 1. Family History Library Film 803005, Roll M653_5, Image 384.

1860 Naval Academy Register: Graduating Class of 1860. Annapolis: United States Naval Academy.

Evans, Charles M. *War of the Aeronauts: A History of Ballooning in the Civil War.* Mechanicsville, PA: Stackpole Books, 2002.

Extracts from the journal of Lieut J. N. Maffitt, C. S. Navy, commanding C. S. S. Florida, May-Dec 31, 1862. Mobile: Confederate States Navy Research Center.

Florida in the Civil War. Florida Department of State, Division of Historical Resources.

Garofalo, Robert, and Mark Elrod. *Civil War Bands.* www.civilwarpoetry.org.

Garrison, Webb. *Civil War Curiosities: Strange Stories, Oddities, Events, and Coincidences.* Nashville: Rutledge Hill, 1994.

———. *More Civil War Curiosities.* Nashville: Rutledge Hill, 1995.

Hanger, James. *Record of Services.* Written for his daughter Alice on her application to the United Daughters of the Confederacy, March 1914.

Harriet Bailey Bullock Daniel Papers (1857-1933). #1361. Oxford, NC: Manuscript Department, William R. Perkins Library, Duke University.

Hayward, James B. *What My Confederate Ancestor Did During the Civil War.* August 25, 1986.

Headley, John W. *The Secret Service of the Confederacy.* www.civil-warsignals.org.

Hébert, Keith S. "Emma Sansom (Johnson)." *Encyclopedia of Alabama.*

A History of the Early Patent Office. Appendix, No. 155, March 23, 1863.

Ingraham, Chris. *Enabling the Human Spirit: The J. E. Hanger Story.* Word Association, 2003.

Intelligence in the Civil War. Washington, DC: Central Intelligence Agency, 2008. https://www.cia.gov/library/publications/additional-publications/civil-war/p25.htm.

Jones, J. William, ed. *Southern Historical Society Papers* 33 (September 20, 1905).

Lawrence, Robert D. *The History of Bill Yopp.* Atlanta: 1920.

Letters of John Whitfield Newton Doak from Camp Davies. Ohio Valley Civil War Association.

"Letters From Veterans." *Confederate Veteran* 2 (August 1894): 227.

Mandes, Thomas C. "Blacks, Jews fight on side of the South." *Washington Times*, June 15, 2002.

The Medical and Surgical History of the Civil War. Vol. 12, *Statistics for the Union Army.*

National Archives and Records Administration. U.S. Passport Applications, Roll 0308, Certificates 25101-25700, May 31 1916-June 6, 1916.

Owen, Thomas M. *Emma Sansom: An Alabama Heroine.* Birmingham, 1904.

Patterson, Mary Kate. Letter. *Confederate Veteran* 4 (February 1896).

"The Pirates Off New England." *Harper's Weekly* (July 11, 1863): 441.

Pittman, Charles. *Ten Cent Bill.* Mustang, OK: Tate, 2008.

Powell, William S. *Dictionary of North Carolina Biography.* Vol. 5, *P-S.* Chapel Hill: University of North Carolina Press, 1994.

Price, William H. *Civil War Handbook.* Fairfax, VA: L. B. Prince, 1961.

Read, C. W. "Reminiscences of the Confederate States Navy." *Southern Historical Society Papers* 1, no. 5 (May 1876).

Read, Joe. "Captain Charlie Read of the Confederate Navy." *Our Heritage.* McComb, MS: 1928.

Rodenbough, Theo. F. "History of the Tenth New York Cavalry." *Photographic History of the Civil War.* Vol. 2. Blue and Grey.

Russell, William. *Cracker: The Story of Florida's Confederate Cow Cavalry.*

Shaw, David W. *Sea Wolf of the Confederacy: The Daring Civil War Raids of Naval Lt. Charlie W. Read.* Dobbs Ferry, NY: Sheridan House, 2005.

Shiloh National Military Park. National Park Service. www.nps.gov.

Signals for the Use of the Navy of the Confederate States. Washington, DC: Operational Archives Branch, Naval Historical Center.

Simonhoff, Harry. *Saga of American Jewry, 1865-1914: Links of an Endless Chain.* Arco, 1959.

Skinner, Martha Sue. "History of the Florida Cow Cavalry." Address to the Hillsborough Community College History Department, March 23, 2003.

Smith, Debra West. *Yankees on the Doorstep: The Story of Sarah Morgan.* Gretna, LA: Pelican, 2001.

Sorrells, Nancy. "James Edward Hanger." *News Leader*, Staunton, VA.

Spedale, William. *The Battle of Baton Rouge: 1862.* Baton Rouge: Land and Land, 1985.

Standen, Iain. *Flags, Lanterns, Rockets and Wires: Signalling in the American Civil War.* www.civilwarsignals.org.

Stern, Philip Van Doren. *The Confederate Navy: A Pictorial History.* Garden City, NY: Doubleday, 1962.

Sutherland, Daniel E. "Jayhawkers and Bushwhackers." *Encyclopedia of Arkansas.*

Taylor, Robert A. "Cow Cavalry: Munnerlyn's Battalion in Florida, 1864-1865." *The Florida Historical Quarterly* 65, no. 2 (October 1986).

Thompson, Holland. "The Prisons of the Civil War." *Photographic History of the Civil War.* Vol. 4, *Soldier Life and Secret Service, Prisons and Hospitals.* Blue and Grey, 1987.

Thompson, Scott. *Fifty Who Made a Difference: Contributions of African Americans to Laurens County and Beyond.* Laurens County Historical Society, 2009.

———. *A History of Dublin and Laurens County, Georgia.* Laurens

County Historical Society, 2009."A Tribute to Their Arduous and Invaluable Services During the War." *Charleston Sunday News,* May 2, 1897.

"A True Heroine." *Jacksonville Republican*, May 9, 1863.

Ward, Patricia Spain. *Simon Baruch: Rebel in the Ranks of Medicine, 1840-1921.* Tuscaloosa: University of Alabama Press, 1994.

Williston, E. C. *Recollections of Buck* (Dr. William Minor Bryan, Capt. John Bryan's son, 1882-1934).

Wooster, Ralph A. "Civil War." *Handbook of Texas Online.* Texas State Historical Association.

Wyeth, John Allan. *Life of Lieutenant-General Nathan Bedford Forrest.* New York: Harper and Brothers, 1908.

Wynne, Lewis, and Robert Taylor. *Florida in the Civil War.* Charleston: Arcadia, 2001.

Yeary, Mamie. *Reminiscences of the Boys in Gray, 1861-1865.* Dallas: Smith and Lamar, 1912.

Young, Bennett H. *Confederate Wizards of the Saddle.* 1914. Reprint, Kennesaw, GA: Continental, 1958.

Index